Blanche Lucile Macdonell

Diane of Ville Marie

A Romance of French Canada

Blanche Lucile Macdonell

Diane of Ville Marie
A Romance of French Canada

ISBN/EAN: 9783744772006

Printed in Europe, USA, Canada, Australia, Japan

Cover: Foto ©Andreas Hilbeck / pixelio.de

More available books at **www.hansebooks.com**

A ROMANCE OF FRENCH CANADA.

BY

BLANCHE LUCILE MACDONELL.

WILLIAM BRIGGS,

29-33 RICHMOND ST. WEST.

MONTREAL: C. W. COATES.   HALIFAX: S. F. HUESTIS.

1898

IN LOVING MEMORY OF

A Mother

WHO WAS

INSPIRATION, FRIEND AND COMFORTER.

PREFACE.

THIS story is an attempt to make known the men and women who once lived and loved and suffered amid these very scenes wherein we are now enacting our own life stories.

In dealing with historical events and characters it seems only fair to the reader to avow what liberties have been taken with facts, and to state exactly to what extent this tale is founded upon history.

The Le Ber family were prominent figures among their contemporaries. Jacques Le Ber, brother-in-law to the redoubtable Charles Le Moyne, was one of the richest merchants of New France. A hardy and intrepid soldier, he was ennobled by Louis XIV. in 1696. In speaking of him M. Dollier de Casson says: "M. Jacques Le Ber has in this way rendered valuable services to the colony, exposing himself very often in canoe, on the ice, or in the woods, carrying despatches."

His only daughter, Jeanne Le Ber, was considered

a great heiress. At seventeen she determined to offer herself as an expiatory offering for the sins of her country. During the fifteen years following she remained in seclusion in her father's house, and was never seen but once, and that exactly as described in this story. Later, this fair enthusiast decided to give the Sisters of the Congregation sufficient money to build their church, if they would provide her a cell behind the altar in which she could spend the remainder of her days. This cell, divided into three storeys, and extending the whole length of the building, was from ten to twelve feet deep.

The original deed, containing these conditions— drawn up by Bassett, a notary of Ville Marie, and signed by the principal nuns of the Congregation, as well as by M. Dollier de Casson, Superior of the Seminary—may still be seen in the Registrar's office in Montreal.

The Le Ber family proved substantial benefactors to the Sisters of the Congregation. Pierre Le Ber the eldest son, left them a legacy of two thousand francs, and his sister remembered them handsomely.

Pierre Le Ber joined Charon de la Barre in founding L' Institut des Frères Hospitaliers de Ville Marie. He was the only one of Charon's associates who remained faithful to the end. He appears to have been the first Canadian artist, and painted portraits of le Sieur Bourgeois, St. Paul, Ste. Thérèse, and the Virgin Mary, for different churches. He died in 1707, and his heart was buried in the Church of the Congregation.

Lydia Longloy, a New England girl, was taken prisoner by the Abenaquis in 1694. She was baptized a Roman Catholic in Ville Marie on April 14th, 1696.

The Chevalier de Crisasi was a veritable personage. Charlevoix says of this gentleman: "One does not know which to admire most, his skill in war, his sagacity in council, his fertility of resource, or his presence of mind in action." The elder brother, the Marquis de Crisasi, was appointed Governor of Three Rivers; the Chevalier, neglected by his friends and forgotten by the Court, died of a broken heart.

Madame de Monesthrol, her niece, and Nanon can lay no claim to be considered historical, but have been drawn after close and extensive study of the types portrayed in the histories and memoirs of the time.

It may be objected that the expedition of Diane and Lydia to Mount Royal is improbable; but it must be remembered the road to the Mountain furnished the most popular pilgrimage of that period, and the dangers which beset the enterprise only heightened its merits. At a still earlier date Madame d'Aillebout and her sister climbed the mountain-side nine days in succession in order to make a neuvena before the cross erected by Maisonneuve.

Four Iroquois were actually burned at Montreal in the manner described, but the event occurred in 1701. Dubocq's exploit is likewise historically correct, but it also occurred some years later than I have taken the liberty of placing it. In these, as in some other instances, the actual chronology has not been strictly followed, but has been altered to suit the exigencies of the tale.

BLANCHE LUCILE MACDONELL.

CONTENTS.

CONTENTS.

DIANE OF VILLE MARIE.

CHAPTER I.

THE SEIGNIORY OF SENNEVILLE.

A LANGUID summer day was that of the 3rd of
August, 1690. A light mist lay like a veil
upon the St. Lawrence, spreading out in grand and
generous swell, the Lake of Two Mountains glimmer-
ing in the distance like a silver shield. The eye
lingered on noble heights, sunny slopes and deep
forest glooms. Near the shore grasses leaned over
the surface of the stream, rushes tall and straight
waved with the ripples, but from their tangled and
interlacing fibres the water flowed clear. The St.
Lawrence was full of tinkling tremors of sound. The
distant hills showed blue and vague through the
fluctuating haze.

At the Seigniory of de Senneville this was a busy
time. The Seignior, Jacques Le Ber, had been super-
intending the gathering of his harvests. A far-
sighted and thrifty man in business affairs, while
the whole colony existed in a state of extreme
penury he had contrived to accumulate great wealth.
To him the New World had proved wonderfully

profitable. The Western fur trade had led to fortune. Indomitable energy and sound judgment aided him to overcome the difficulties under which the new country labored, while experience, joined to natural shrewdness, taught how to steer safely between the varying official interests which in turn directed the colony.

The ravages of the caterpillars had left little harvest to gather, and had it not been for the marvellous incursion of squirrels, which fairly swarmed over the land, many of the people must have starved. Broken, uneven fields stretched to the borders of the forest. Amidst the stumps and prostrate trees of the unsightly clearing, the colonists pursued their labors, protected by a body of regulars whom the merchants had brought from Ville Marie. At short distances sentinels were posted to give the alarm at any sign of approaching danger.

These were troublous times for the handful of French settlers scattered amidst the savage hordes and half-reclaimed forests of the New World. Amid tangled thickets and deep ravines, in the shade and stillness of columned woods, behind woody islets, everywhere there lurked danger and terror. The fierce and cruel Iroquois were on the war-path. These tireless savages owed their triumphs as much to craft as to their extraordinary boldness and bravery. They rarely approached the settlements in winter, when the trees and bushes had no leaves to conceal their advance, and when their movements would be betrayed by the track of their snowshoes, but they were always to be expected at the time of sowing and harvest, when it was possible to do the most mischief.

Scarcely one of the little party collected at Senneville but had passed through scenes of grim horror. Though they chattered over their work with true Gallic light-heartedness and vivacity, most of them could have related experiences of the unsleeping hatred and cruelty of the Iroquois and the hardships of forest life.

Only two years before, Louison Guimond's young brother had been butchered before her eyes, and with the remains of the mutilated body the dazed and miserable woman had journeyed alone through the wilderness to secure Christian burial for her dead. Sans Quartier, an old soldier, returning from an expedition, had found his home in ashes and his young wife and child carried away captive. Another soldier, Frap d'Abord, held his musket awkwardly (though none could do better service) because his finger had been burned in the bowl of an Indian pipe, one of the many ingenious forms of torture practised by the Iroquois. Baptiste Bras de Fer, a hardy Canadian voyageur and coureur de bois, could tell true tales of peril and adventure in the pathless forest, such as chilled the blood in the listener's veins—stories of forced marches through sodden snowdrifts and matted thickets, over rocks and cliffs and swollen streams, when men, perishing from cold and famine, boiled moccasins for food, and scraped away the snow in search of beech and hickory nuts. The resignation born of long usage, the conviction that these conditions were beyond remedy, that the only thing to be done was to endure, enabled these people to assume a demeanor of calmness and patience. But there was always an hysterical quiver in Louison's shrill laughter. When Sans Quartier was silent the lines of pain deepened in his stern, bronzed face ; the very name of an Indian was sufficient to make Frap d'Abord swear long strings of queer, quaint oaths. Nevertheless their chatter usually flowed on cheerily, with much merriment and little complaint.

The scanty harvests had been gathered, and the party, with the exception of Gregoire and his wife, Goulet the farmer, and the soldiers left to garrison the fort, prepared for their return to Ville Marie. Though the distance to be traversed was not great, the journey was both toilsome and perilous. In order to escape the turmoil of the Lachine Rapids the canoes had to be shouldered through the forest. The large flat-bottomed boats, being too heavy for such handling, were to be dragged and pushed in the shallow water close to the bank by gangs of men, who toiled and struggled amidst rocks and foam. Just now the danger and inconvenience of transit were considerably increased by the presence of some of the ladies of the Le Ber household who had accompanied the party to Senneville.

Shrewd trader and fearless soldier as was the honest merchant of Ville Marie, he possessed a knightly spirit and had never yet been able to refuse a request urged by his ward, Diane de Monesthrol. When that capricious damsel had determined to accompany the harvesting expedition, and had persuaded Le Ber's nephew, Le Moyne de St. Helène, and his young wife (who as Jeanne de Fresnoy Carion had also been Le Ber's ward,) to join it, it was perfectly understood in the household that opposition was useless, and the merchant, against his better judgment, yielded to the girl's pretty coaxing.

" Throw your tongue to the dogs—of what use to argue with our demoiselle ; she has always ten answers to one objection. One fine day she, and we others tied to her heels, will furnish an excellent meal to those sorcerers of Iroquois—faith of Nanon Benest ! " cried Madame de Monesthrol's serving-woman, with the freedom of a faithful and attached French servant.

Jacques Le Ber stood close to the shore, where the men, shouting and joking, were loading the boats. His was a round, bourgeois, somewhat heavy type of face, seamed and tanned by work and weather, deco-rated by a slight moustache, and redeemed from commonness by bright, earnest eyes. He wore a three-cornered hat, and over his ample shoulders was spread a stiff white collar of wide expanse and studied plainness. He looked what he was, a well-to-do citizen of good renown and sage deportment.

At Diane de Monesthrol's approach he turned hastily. A true and earnest friendship united the busy trader and this young girl of noble birth. No young cavalier (and Diane was said to be the fairest demoiselle in New France) appreciated the fairness of her gracious youth more thoroughly than the world-worn elderly man whose thoughts were engrossed with so many pressing material interests. His most soothing consolations for several years past had come from this eager-eyed, girlish creature who seemed intuitively to comprehend his feelings.

In the midst of his prosperity the merchant had experienced heavy bereavements. He had lost his wife, the thoughtful and sympathetic partner of all his interests. When their only daughter in the early promise of her youth had resolved to withdraw into absolute seclusion, and devote herself as a public offering to God for the sins of her country, spiritual pride had induced him to consent to the sacrifice. He had been assured by his guides in religion that he and his wife were to serve as models to all the parents in the colony; they would be honored as was Abraham for his sacrifice of Isaac.

Still, even with that consolation, the sundering of domestic ties lay heavily on his heart. In the sober wisdom that came with years of disappointment, through the dark experiences that usually isolate men's thoughts, he had found comfort in the frank, simple, and guileless spirit of the girl to whom he had afforded protection. In reality the man had two natures: the one practical, ambitious, worldly, which was known to all the world; the other, rarely suspected, was ideal and passionate, and throve apart from all the common requirements of life.

The primeval strength and freshness of a new world, as yet uncontaminated by the vices of advanced civilization, seemed to have breathed into this girl an abounding energy which resulted in a rare union of vigor and native delicacy. The transplanted flower had not lost the charm distinctive of her class, and had gained in spirit and character. The warmth of the sunlight, the flush of youth, the fresh breeze of the springtide had crystallized within her. The glory of this undiscovered country, full of grand perils and deliverances, storms to be braved, griefs, joys and labors to be lived through, were in the highest degree congenial to her dauntless temperament.

As they made ready to start, Le Ber's eyes rested with satisfied gaze upon the radiant beauty of his young ward. Her complexion was purely pale; the delicately-cut features, lit up by that undisturbed equanimity which is the inheritance of vigorous minds, were piquant rather than regular. The cheeks were beautified by playful dimples, the short upper lip was fresh as a rose, while the softly-rounded and mutinous chin indicated reserve forces of strength as yet scarcely suspected. Madame de Monesthrol sometimes lamented that according to the canons of taste her niece's eyes ought to have been brown, yet in defiance of all rule they were intensely blue, and shaded by black heavy curling lashes. Her hair, lightly powdered, was partly crimped and partly curled. Her gown of dark cloth opened at the throat, which was veiled by a lace kerchief; a long waisted corsage fitted tightly over the bust, and flounces of lace finished off the under-skirt and fell from the sleeves. The regard which Diane turned on the world was the frank, friendly and confiding look of a child; mischievous often it might be, scornful sometimes at the sight of anything mean or paltry, yet always the simple gaze of a soul as yet undisturbed by passion or distrust.

"And it has been pleasant to have me with you?" the girl asked, taking her guardian's arm, and looking up smilingly into his face.

The wrinkles under Le Ber's deep-set eyes and the tense lines about his mouth relaxed in an indulgent smile.

"That goes without saying, my little one; your presence carries sunshine. We must remember, how-ever, the nerves of Madame la Marquise, who will doubtless await your return with anxiety. If we would reach Ville Marie by daylight it is time to start; and not to succeed in doing so would expose us to many dangers. Nanon has at last completed her preparations. St. Hélène is anxious to be gone; experience has taught him the perils of delay. Nor shall I feel at rest until I see you within the walls of the town."

CHAPTER II.

A FORTIFIED RESIDENCE.

"I SHOULD like the Indians to know that we understand the use of the paddle! I don't absolutely deny that these savages possess some skill in constructing a canoe; but, I ask you, have they the address to give it the daintiness of form which renders ours so coquettish as they dance upon the water? This is not a canoe—it is a feather—a bird that skims the air—a cloud chased by the wind—it should fly! You may see what marvels of swiftness that of M. du Chesne will perform directly." So spoke a tall Canadian, whose skill as a boatman had gained him the title of "le Canotier."

Madame de St. Helène stood cloaked and hooded in black lace, an elegant, dignified figure whose appearance savored too much of the refinement of urban life to be in harmony with this rustic scene. Her two little children, attended by servants, were beside her.

"I would we were safe within the shelter of Ville Marie," she said wistfully. "Once we quit the stone walls of the fort who can say what trouble may assail us."

"Oh! for that, trouble comes soon enough; it is not worth our while to search for it, Jeanne," her husband returned lightly. "The question now to be considered is our immediate start. Why, I wonder, do we linger?"

The canoes were ready. Soldiers and workmen gathered around them looking expectantly toward the fort. Among these a woman pushed her way, scolding, laughing, gesticulating. Nanon was a comely woman of her class, strong and thick-set, with a face full of piquancy and vivacity. Brown as a berry was this daughter of southern France, with red cheeks and eyes black as sloes. She wore a brown petticoat, a crimson apron with a bib, and a coquettish lace cap with hanging lappets. At every vehement movement her long gold earrings quivered and jingled.

"Behold! Madame, Mademoiselle and these gentlemen all are accommodated, and I but attend the good pleasure of the Sieur du Chesne," she protested in high, shrill tones.

"Eh, corbleu! but no, this good Nanon awaits no convenience of mine," remonstrated a laughing boyish voice; "there is place in the craft of Sans Quartier for thee, my girl. Diane has promised to share my canoe, father," turning to Le Ber, who stood by an amused listener, "and I have no hesitation in wagering that it is we who shall reach Lachine first."

"Hein, no!" Nanon reduced her forehead to an inch of tight cords, crossed her arms, and shook

herself from side to side in the most approved style
of obstinacy. " I have morals, me, even in the wilderness. It is necessary to remember *les convenances*.
In our country ladies are guarded under the care of
their mothers, as the hen gathers her chickens under
her wings. My demoiselle has been confided to my
care by Madame la Marquise ; not a step, not a
shadow of a step, moves my young lady without my
attendance. Madame counts upon my faith."

" It is I who am responsible to Madame la Marquise for Mademoiselle de Monesthrol ; nor is it
likely that surrounded by friends any harm will befall
her. Your faithful attachment to your mistress, my
girl, alone excuses the presumption of your inter-
ference. Du Chesne, you will take charge of Diane ;
Jean and Nanon will follow closely in the larger
canoe ; we shall all remain in sight of one another."
Thus Le Ber decisively settled the question ; then,
holding his hat under his arm, with a profound bow
he offered his hand to conduct Madame de St. Helène
to the boat.

" Now, are you satisfied?" the young man laughed
gaily. " Diane, is it not a joke? You and I surely
might be allowed to take care of ourselves."

Nanon was still disposed to be nettled ; she
resented Le Ber's rebuke, but no one could ever
resist the gay confidence of the trader's youngest son.

Jean Le Ber du Chesne might fitly serve as an
example of the best type of the colonial youth of the
period. Born and nurtured in Canada, thoroughly

versed in wood-craft, seasoned to toil, fatigue and trying extremes of climate, trained amidst dangers and alarms, while yet in his teens he had acquired a reputation for tact and courage. As the sea is the sailor's native element, his cherished career, his passion, so was the forest that of Le Ber du Chesne. From childhood he had accompanied his cousins, the Le Moynes, a family of heroes, upon the most difficult and arduous expeditions. In the elastic buoyancy of early youth, hardship and perils had but developed an uncommon vitality and afforded opportunities for the display of resource and valor. The austerity of the most sombre acetic relaxed at the sight of his debonair face; the craftiest of Indian diplomats, the most lawless of coureurs de bois were alike moulded to the purposes of the young Canadian.

"We shall keep Bibelot with us. Diane and I have no desire to furnish *bouillon à l'Iroquois*; we should neither of us relish being thrown into the kettle." Du Chesne's gay inadvertent laugh rang out as he jested with one of the grimmest terrors of colonial life.

Three soldiers rowed the larger craft, occupied by Le Ber and St. Hélène with the wife and children of the latter. Several other boats followed, carrying servants, soldiers, workpeople and baggage.

"Hasten, then, my son; follow us closely." Le Ber looked around anxiously. "It is but three years, remember, since Senneville was last attacked by the Iroquois. What has been may happen again. It is the policy of the savages to attack stragglers. Above all things it is necessary to keep together."

The oars were raised high in the air, and as they moved a shower of crystal drops flashed in the sunlight. At the same time the voices of the boatmen broke out into a lusty chorus which rang cheerily across the water :

> " Y'a-t il un étang.
> Fringue, Fringue sur l'aviron.
> Trois beaux canards
> S'en vont baignants
> Fringue, Fringue sur la rivière
> Fringue, Fringue sur l'aviron."

Du Chesne was holding the canoe into which Diane was about to step when there arose an outcry from the fort.

" Monsieur! Monsieur! Sieur du Chesne!" It was Nanon, her plump figure quivering with excitement, who called in hot haste. " It is that snake of a Gouillon who disputes with the soldiers. Hasten, then, ere there is murder done."

" But an instant, Diane. That lazy varlet lives but to do mischief—just when we are in haste, too. But he shall pay for his pleasure this time."

Diane remained alone upon the shore, watching the rapidly disappearing party, gaily waving a bright-hued silken scarf as long as they were in sight. Gentle fancies, floating vaguely through her mind without ever assuming definite form, were reflected on her face in lines of exquisite sweetness; her delicately

fanciful maiden dreams inspired no yearning for
future bliss, but only perfect satisfaction with the
present. The voyage down the river would be one
continuous pleasure. She and the young man were
close comrades and firm friends. Being very young
when his mother died, the affectionate lad had
grieved deeply. In his loneliness it was his young
playmate who had come nearest to his heart; she had
taken the place of the sister whom religious enthusiasm had estranged from all human interests.
Diane had become his warmest sympathizer, the
confidante of countless escapades. The girl, on her
part, was conscious that the serenity of the blue sky,
the tender greenness and stillness of the landscape,
all seemed to borrow a new charm when viewed in
his company.

The Seigniory had once been called Boisbriant,
after the first grantee, Sidrac de Gui, Sieur de Briant,
but when it passed into Le Ber's possession, it was
renamed Senneville. It was a post of considerable
strategic value. The fort, built at the end of the
Island of Montreal, where the St. Lawrence and
Ottawa Rivers joined, offered effectual protection
against the attacks of the Iroquois, and was of great
service to the colony.

In front the Ottawa flowed, through its picturesque
and fertile islands, while on the other side the St.
Lawrence rolled like a river of gold. A little to the
north-west the water expanded into the Lake of Two
Mountains, the twin peaks which gave it their name

appearing in the hazy distance. On Ile St. Paul Le
Ber had erected large storehouses. On Ile Perrot
stood a cluster of buildings constructed by Le Ber's
rival and antagonist, Perrot, the ex-Governor of Ville
Marie, in order to intercept the Indian tribes from the
upper lakes on their way to the annual fair at Montreal. Ile Perrot was the rendezvous of soldiers who
had escaped from the restraints of a harsh discipline
to the freedom of the woods, and of rovers of every
description outlawed by the royal edict.

The fort at Senneville was remarkably well built ;
the material of rough boulder stones, with stone jambs,
lintel sills and fire-places. The buildings formed a
parallelogram of which the residence was one end, the
sides being simply defensive walls, nowhere more than
twelve feet high, pierced with loopholes and having a
gateway. At the angles stood flanking towers, the
first two being connected with a wall which did not
come much above the first floor window. The courtyard was nearly square, measuring about eighty feet
each way, and looking north-west across the Lake of
Two Mountains.

The residential part had a frontage of about eighty
feet and a depth of thirty-five. In front it was two
stories in height, but, as the ground was higher inside
the courtyard, at the back it was only a story and a
half. It had a high pitched roof, tall chimneys and
wide fire-places. The walls of the towers were
strengthened by an outward spread at the base. The
towers measured only about twelve feet square inside ;

they were two and a half stories in height and had large windows in their outer walls, and on the sides, commanding the main walls, small embrasures were mounted with light artillery.

In addition to the castle proper there were out-buildings which served more than one purpose. A few hundred yards back from the river the ground swelled to a gently wooded height, crowned by a fortified windmill. These picturesque structures were a distinctive feature in the landscape throughout all New France and did good service in protecting the settlers. The mill at Senneville possessed rather an unusual adjunct, a hooded door which served the same purpose as the machicolations of a mediæval castle. The tower was three stories in height, and measured fifteen feet inside, the floor being supported by strong oak beams. The chimney was simply a flue in the thickness of the wall opening to the outer air just below the second story ceiling; the hood opened before the floor of the same chamber. The roof was of conical form, covered with shingles, the latter always a point of weakness in time of attack.

Nature here on every side unfolded panoramic views of loveliness. Flickers of light were reflected in the water; trailing vines festooned the trees. There were quiet marshes golden with swaying grasses, and, farther away, sombre masses of pine through which opened mysterious shadowy vistas.

CHAPTER III.

AN IROQUOIS ATTACK.

DESPITE the beauty of the scene just described, Bibelot, the dog, was plainly dissatisfied with the existing order of things. She was a direct descendant of Pilot, one of a number of dogs sent from France to Ville Marie shortly after its foundation in order to assist the brave colonists in their warfare against the Indians. Detesting the savages by instinct, these trusty animals were invaluable in detecting ambuscades. Bibelot now ran here and there, her bushy tail raised high and curled like a feather over her back, her slender, alert head and bright eyes full of keen interest, sniffing among the grass and branches as though solicitous of some trail of fox or rabbit. Game abounded in the woods ; from where she stood Diane could see a great herd of elk defile quietly between the water and the forest.

The dog's persistent uneasiness attracted Diane's attention. Suddenly the long-drawn, melancholy cry of a water-fowl fell upon her ear. The sound might have passed unheeded by faculties less keen and highly strung ; but as she started at the cry, Bibelot, throwing back her head and quivering all over with rage, uttered a low, deep growl. The call was repeated several times. Could it be a signal? The dog's excitement seemed to warrant the supposition. As she gazed apprehensively about her, the trunk of a fallen tree, lying on the ground close at hand, seemed to Diane to stir. Was imagination playing her false? The girl had grown up amidst the constant dangers of the adventurous colonial life. She knew well that the Iroquois roamed through the deserted settlements and prowled continually around the forts. No one could account for the mysterious movements of these agile warriors, nor for the subtilty and malice of their stratagems. She now stood perfectly still as if she were a figure painted on the pale green background. The heart beat high in her breast, the color came and went in her cheek. A gray squirrel with small bright eyes scudded through the grass close beside her. At that instant the log moved again, this time with a hasty, impulsive jerk. There was no doubt but that in the hollow trunk an Indian lay concealed. Immediately the loud clamor of Bibelot's bark rang out, clear and distinct. Quick as a gleam of light the forest was alive with shadowy figures moving stealthily and silently among the trees. Diane saw that her only chance of escape lay in immediate action, and that the lives of those in the fort might depend upon her presence of mind. She understood but too well the nameless horrors which captivity among the savages meant—death was nothing in comparison.

" *Aux armes ! aux armes !* " the girlish voice rang
out in clear, piercing tones. Bibelot's resounding
howls were lost in the din as the Indians, uttering
their appalling yells, dashed towards her. Like an
arrow from a bow, fleet as a young fawn, Diana sprang
forward, several of the dusky braves starting in hot
pursuit. She had some advantage of distance in the
start, but so close were her pursuers that the slightest
hesitation, a false step, a slip on the sun-burnt grass,
would prove fatal. The footsteps of her foremost
pursuer fell with growing clearness upon her ears.
With every muscle strained to its utmost tension on
she flew, all the while conscious that the foe was
steadily gaining upon her. She had almost reached
the threshold of the fort when, shouting his own
name in the Indian fashion, the Iroquois stretched
out his hand to grasp her shoulder. She could feel
the touch of his fingers upon the lace border of the
kerchief she wore around her neck. At this instant
the report of a pistol rang out. With a sharp, convulsive shudder the savage sprang high in the air and
fell prostrate to the ground, as Diane, breathless and
trembling, was drawn into the fort by du Chesne.

A prescient excitement blazed in the young man's
eyes. His spirited face was full of resolution and
confidence.

"Fear not, Diane," he said, as he barricaded the
door, "there are not a great number of Iroquois
gathered outside, and they rarely attack a fort. Our
most serious danger is that the sound of the guns

may induce my father to return, and that from the shore they will fire upon the boats. We are safe enough here, but we must not allow them to suspect that our garrison is so small. I have already posted the men ; we can only await the attack."

Diane sank down faint and sick, yet with a sweet consolatory thought underlying her physical weakness. Whatever might happen she would not be obliged to endure alone ; she could depend upon a sympathy and companionship she highly prized.

"And Jean, where is he ? " du Chesne continued, as though he wished to give her time to recover herself. "*Pasembleau!* that lazy varlet has no heart for fighting ; that I'll swear. Nanon, thou canst manage an arquebus as well as any man among them. My brave girl, we will need thy help."

Nanon's black eyes darted furious glances as she ground her teeth in sheer wrath.

"Yes, Monsieur, I am capable of that, and may I put an end to one of these sorcerers, these brigands, with every shot I fire ! My hairs are all rubbed the wrong way at the sight of these wolves. Chut ! Mademoiselle, why so pale ? I think little of these affairs, me ; still there is no laughing under the nose when it relates to the Iroquois. Sit far back if you would not see, and for a high-born demoiselle I grant—"

"No, Nanon," Diane interposed, repulsing the well-intentioned offers of assistance. "Whatever befalls the others I share, since our lot has been cast together."

With an exultant throb the girl's spirit leaped free from its chains. Amidst these perilous circumstances she was conscious of feeling a perfect courage and serenity. Turning his head, du Chesne smiled at her tone.

"Place yourself behind me, Diane; you can help by loading as I fire. We will stand on our defence. These wolves will lurk about and try to climb into the fort under the cover of darkness. We must not permit them to approach, lest they set fire to the roof."

The Iroquois showed no disposition to retire, but commenced industriously to erect barricades of stones and bushes, as though notwithstanding the check they had encountered they were resolved to begin a prolonged siege.

"It looks as though it may be late before we reach Ville Marie. B-r-r-r-r! The tongue of our good Nanon goes like the clapper of a mill. Well, she amuses the soldiers, and she is as ready to aid with the hands as the voice. These savages take us for targets, do they? When the violins play, then is the time to dance."

Bibelot kept up a continuous barking, which added to the tumult. Nanon's wrathful denunciations of the enemy delighted the soldiers and soothed her own nerves, even if they failed to annihilate the assailants. Thus the little party contrived to keep up their spirits.

Diane, keeping close behind du Chesne, loading one gun as he fired another, standing ready to obey his behests, had time to think of many things. Her eyes rested upon the young man with growing amazement. It was an hour of revelation. All the careless boyishness of his face had been replaced by an expression keen, stern, resolute; his eyes flamed with a light which was almost cruel in its intensity. There was something splendid in the stalwart pride of courage. Watching this novel moulding of the familiar features, the girl was beset by a strange sense of unreality. This was no longer her boyish comrade whom she had teased and flattered and cajoled; this was a man strong to command, to defy fate, who would rise equal to every crisis, and who would grow with every emergency. An absorbing feeling took possession of Diane's mind, her heart swelled with a new spring of impassioned emotion, a subtle intoxication mounted like fire to her brain. It dawned upon her that du Chesne was a hero, and that he had counted her worthy of aiding him in his extremity. This thought flushed her horizon with the sunshine of heroic impulse. Her face was full of a tense eagerness, almost beyond the artifices of concealment. Once speaking, she ventured rather breathlessly:

"Gentlemen are born to shed their blood for God and the King."

"That goes without saying," he replied quietly. Du Chesne had had so much experience of Indian warfare that he accepted encounters such as this as a matter of course. "When the end has to come, a day sooner or later, what does it matter?" Then his buoyant temperament reasserting itself, he added,

"Bah! Diane, our hour is not yet. You looked so pale and so serious you made me almost shiver. This is but a brush with these wolves. Very different would it be were we out in the open, far from the protection of the fort; then would there be occasion for grimaces. What is that? Look, Diane!" Then his voice rose in a glad cry. His keen eyes had discovered a swarm of canoes, thick as a flight of blackbirds in autumn, on the waters of the Ottawa.

"Aid is at hand! I was not sure that this might not be a reinforcement of Iroquois, in which case we were lost; but no, these are our own allies. Saved! Do you hear, Diane? Saved!"

Diane sank on her knees. Her face shone with that spiritual light with which at moments of supreme feeling the soul illumines its earthly tenement.

"The good Lord has saved us from the hands of our enemies." The girl could have wept with thankfulness and delight, but controlled herself by an effort.

"Aye, and our lady of Bonsecours shall have three as fine waxen tapers burning before her shrine as money can buy, and that before the week is out," Nanon protested excitedly. "I make no clamor for all the world to hear, like that vulture Mam'selle Anne, but I make my religion all the same. Never could I believe that the holy saints could be so ungrateful and inconsiderate as to refuse to listen to the prayers of my demoiselle."

CHAPTER IV.

AN ENGLISH CAPTIVE.

SUDDENLY the air was filled with yells as, leaping from their canoes and advancing through a ridge of thick forest beyond the open fields, scores of half-naked savages swarmed into the clearing. Ensconced behind the ramparts of the fort, the little band watched the proceedings in silence. Through the leafy arches of the woods, over hill and hollow, across still swamp and gurgling brook, rang the war-whoops of the new arrivals as they rushed upon their hereditary foes.

"It is now the turn of the wolves to dance, and we can assist at the festivities!" exclaimed du Chesne, hilariously. "This is a war party of Hurons and Algonquins returning from an expedition."

The Iroquois, though taken by surprise, fought with courage and address, leaping and dodging among the trees and rocks until at last, finding themselves outnumbered and overborne, they retreated, bearing the wounded and most of their dead with them. As the tumult of the conflict died away, the young Frenchman observed in a tone of satisfaction, "It is settled. Have no apprehensions, Diane; our adversaries have fled, carrying something to remember us by as well."

"Is it, then, quite certain, M'sieur, that they have gone, but beyond doubt," pleaded a timorous voice from some remote depth of obscurity.

"Wretched coward! of much use thou hast been. And where hast thou hidden thy miserable carcase?" returned du Chesne in hot anger.

"Scaramouch! screech-owl! much help thou hast been in saving my demoiselle and me," Nanon mocked one of her most constant admirers. "Oh, that I were entrusted with the wringing of thy unworthy neck.

With an insinuating smile on his sleek, fat face the valet crept out from the dark corner which had afforded him shelter.

"Ouf! that such should exist!" the young commandant cried contemptuously. "Poltroon! art thou not ashamed to show thy face?"

"But, M'sieur du Chesne; figure to yourself—it is quite simple," with an affectation of innocent frankness. "It is the nature of M'sieur to be courageous, to love fighting—it is well. It is the delight of Nanon to chatter. It is Bibelot's instinct to hate the savages; you observe even the smell of one throws her into a frenzy. For me, I have an invincible repugnance to the scalping knife of the Iroquois. Had I permitted myself to be killed M'sieur would have lost a faithful servant, and these pagans would have added a fresh sin to the list of their enormities.

May I ask, M'sieur, is it the duty of good Christians to tempt the heathen? Should they not rather give an example of patience and resignation?"

The new arrivals now claimed attention. Sunburned warriors they were, of tall stalwart build, limbed like statues. Success had crowned their arms, as shown in the imposing array of scalps and the necklaces of ears and fingers which many of them wore. They looked like painted spectres, grotesquely horrible in horns and tails; their faces painted red or green, with black or white spots; their ears and noses hung with ornaments of iron, and their naked bodies daubed with figures of various animals. These fierce, capricious braves smiled upon the fiery young soldier whose courage had long since won their approbation.

"What, my brother, we have arrived in time to strengthen your arm against our foes?" exclaimed the principal war chief. "The face of our white brother is welcome to the eyes of Howaha."

The last time du Chesne had met Howaha was at the annual fair in Ville Marie, when he appeared in a picturesque attire befitting his dignity and rank. He was much less imposing now as he squatted on the grass after his triumphs, chopping rank tobacco with a scalping-knife. An astute old savage, well trained in arts of policy, he showed every disposition to render himself agreeable to the son of the influential French trader.

"But look, du Chesne! Here is a white prisoner —a woman, too. Oh, surely she is not dead!" cried Diane.

"No, not dead, Diane, but evidently overcome by fatigue and fright. Howaha tells me she is a New England girl whom they have taken. She has been given to one of the chiefs, Nitchoua, to replace a wife he lost during the winter. Had it not been for that she would have been butchered on the spot."

"An English heretic! Take care, then, Mademoiselle ; she may have the evil eye. True sorcerers are these English ; it is said they devour little children, even to the bones. No doubt they are wicked, and of a wickedness truly terrible—yet this one has not the appearance of a veritable monster," continued Nanon with wavering positiveness.

In the lethargy of utter exhaustion, her limbs relaxed and nerveless, the girl lay on the grass just as she had been thrown by the Indians. She seemed utterly unconscious of the clamor of voices or of the curious regard directed towards her, as though in the terrible numbness of despair she had grown indifferent to her fate. Her features were delicately formed, her complexion of an exquisite purity, yet so utterly devoid of color that she resembled a beautiful statue rather than a living woman.

Diane, feeling that inexplicable attraction which frequently draws together persons of entirely different natures, examined her closely. The novel sensations and sentiments so recently awakened within her endowed all existence with a new pathos as well as a new delight. She knelt down beside the captive girl, smoothing the flaxen hair which the sunlight turned

35

to gold, clasping the cold, passive hands in her own, whispering soft words of comfort and encouragement. The stranger stared vacantly into the French girl's face, while Diane's brilliant eyes dimmed with the sympathetic moisture of compassion.

"There has been a violent dispute concerning the prisoner," explained du Chesne, who understood the Indian dialects perfectly; "Nitchoua wishes to take her as his wife. Another party want to torture her when they reach their own village, and Howaha has threatened to settle the dispute by a blow with a tomahawk which will terminate at once the discussion and the existence of the captive."

"How beautiful she is! She is already half dead with misery and fatigue; I can scarcely feel her heart beat." A keen compassion pleaded in the intensity of Diane's faltering accents. "You know what captivity among the Indians means. Think of this tender creature submitted to the torture. I should know no rest all the remainder of my life for thinking of it. This might have been our own case had not the Holy Virgin sent us aid. We can never desert her in her extremity—you must find some way of ransoming her, du Chesne—you can surely manage it."

"I do not know. There is the merest pinch of hope; but I will do my best to save her, Diane."

The same thought already had crossed the young man's mind. The chief impression made upon him by this stranger was one of helpless beauty and innocence. He was chivalrous and tender-hearted, yet he compre-

hended that the rescue of the prisoner was secondary
in importance to propitiating these savage allies. In
the one case the fate of an individual depended upon
his exertions ; in the other the fate of the whole settlement might hang in the balance. In their attempts
to resist the encroachments of the Iroquois the French
could not do without the help of the other Indian
tribes. Du Chesne thoroughly understood the art of
dealing with these children of the forest. He could
conform to their customs and flatter them with cour-
teous address. He understood the uncertain, vacillating temper common to all savages. Unsteady as
aspens, fierce as panthers, rent by mad jealousies, they
were a wild crew who changed their intentions with
the veering of the wind, and whose dancing, singing
and yelling might at any moment turn into war-
whoops against each other or against the French.
There were many difficulties to be considered, but the
young Canadian was not easily daunted, and he
determined to make the effort.

Nerving every faculty for the endeavor, the youth
stood forth, his full deep eyes fixed on the savages
with the masterful scrutiny with which a tamer of wild
beasts might regard the ferocious animals committed
to his charge. His dark eyes were aflame ; there was
so much of quiet strength suggested in his bearing
that, as she listened to his glowing words, Diane's
heart beat high with pride. The daughter of a race
of soldiers, she was deeply imbued with admiration
for physical courage. With bold adroitness he assured

Howaha that if his captive had become a subject of dissension among the red-men, he, their white brother, ever ready to oblige his allies, was willing to relieve them of the burden. He imitated the prolonged accents of the savages and addressed them in turn by their respective tribes, bands and families, calling their men of note by name as though he had been born among them. In all he said his voice and gestures answered to the words. The chiefs, silent and attentive, with gaze riveted upon the bowls of their pipes, listened with cool, impartial interest. Plainly the impression made by the young Canadian's eloquence was favorable ; at every pause in his harangue some sign of approval could be detected.

Du Chesne did not, however, gain his object without some trouble. At one moment Nitchoua started forward, brandishing his hatchet in the air, declaring furiously that the prisoner belonged to him by right of war ; rather than waive his claim he would kill her as she lay helpless before them. "Has Nitchoua killed enemies on the war-path? His arm is weary with killing, his eye with counting. The scalps of his enemies ornament the wigwam of the great chief in such number that they shelter it from rain in the stormy night," vaunted the fierce savage, proclaiming his own deeds of valor.

The English maiden was too far spent to be greatly excited by this new menace. She understood neither the French language nor the Indian dialects, even had she been able to control herself sufficiently to listen.

Occurrences had been struck off by time in such quick succession that they seemed like some terrible continuous nightmare—an awful void in which every wretchedness was conceivable, and in which there was neither comfort nor solace to be found. She was not by nature endowed with nerve or courage. Within the last few days she had become familiar with scenes of massacre and pillage; she had seen her home burned to the ground, her relatives butchered before her eyes, had witnessed the cruel torture of friends and neighbors, had endured incredible fatigue, and had realized the uncertainty concerning her own fate. Now the overstrained brain refused to receive fresh impressions, a merciful lethargy deadened sensation. When the excited savage waved his axe above her head, though she believed her last hour had come, even in this extremity she had not sufficient strength to arouse herself. Prompted by some instinct, her blue eyes turned to Diane with a mute agonized appeal. The French girl returned the gaze with a sob of excitement and agitation swelling at her throat.

"We must take care of you, it is our bounden duty —we could not fail you—trust us," she pleaded, unconscious or careless of the fact that the stranger could not know the meaning of her words. There is, however, a language of the soul which the most distraught can comprehend in the face of a great crisis. As she met the kindly glance bent upon her, a ray of comfort penetrated the darkness which had enveloped the captive's spirit; it was like an ethereal stimulant quickening all her powers.

Finally, on the promise of a rich ransom being given, Nitchoua allowed his wrath to be appeased. He began to dance, holding his hands upraised as though apostrophizing the sky. Suddenly he seized his tomahawk, brandished it wildly, and then flung it far from him.

"Thus I throw away my anger," he shouted; "so I cast away my weapons of blood and war. Let the pale-face girl be led away to the wigwams of the French, since my white brother desires it to be so. We are friends forever. Candwish,* we are brothers."

A swift expression of relief, like a flash of light, crossed du Chesne's face. Howaha arose, and with an air of great dignity said:

"My brothers, it is well. Farewell, war; farewell, tomahawk; no longer have we use for you. We have often been fools, henceforth we will learn wisdom. The French are our brothers; Onontio † is our father. Brother, our covenant with you is a silver chain which can neither break nor rust. We are of the race of the Bear, and as long as there is a drop of blood in his veins the bear never yields to force; but the ear of the bear is ever open to the voice of a friend. Take the prisoner, she is yours; do with her what you will."

"The fawn"—du Chesne pointed to Diane, who

---

* *Candwish*—An Indian word signifying comrade.

† *Onontio*—Frontenac.

still clasped the English girl in her arms,—"will adopt the captive as a sister; she will find shelter in the lodges of the French."

"Aye," Howaha added gravely, "the snow-flower will know peace. Shall the bird in its nest dread the wind and tempest? shall the child in the arms of its mother know fear?"

Realizing that the whim of the savages might change like a drift of dry leaves, du Chesne had no idea of resting in false security. "We will seize the opportunity of going down the river with Howaha," he decided promptly.

Later, as they floated down with the current, the Indians chanted their songs of victory, as an accompaniment striking the edges of their paddles against the sides of their bark canoes. First one wild voice raised itself in strange discordant tones, now dropping low, then rising again, anon swelling into shrill yelps in which all the others joined. Among them two Iroquois prisoners stood upright, shouting their own war-songs in proud defiance, like men who knew no fear of torture or death, while from seven poles raised aloft as many fresh scalps fluttered in the evening breeze. Though the vermilion dusk still lingered over Mount Royal, softly purple in the fading light, the moon, pearly and splendid, swung high in the east, accompanied by a vaguely scintillating star at the zenith.

So it came to pass that the Puritan damsel, Lydia Longloy, entered upon a new existence, protected by

Diane de Monesthrol's tender care, succored by the charity of those French papists the very sound of whose name had until now been a terror to her. The only person who appeared dissatisfied with the turn events had taken was Nanon, who grumbled as she told her beads :

"An extra rosary I must say in order to avert the evil eye. It may even be her ill-luck my little mistress is carrying with her in the shape of this English heretic. We have had sufficient of that, we others, when it has landed us among the savages ; and where next—who can tell ? But for our demoiselle it should be another matter ; for her it must be only sunshine."

CHAPTER V.

A CANADIAN HOME.

THE house occupied by Jacques Le Ber in Ville Marie stood at the corner of St. Paul and St. Joseph streets. The front windows commanded a view of the St. Lawrence, while those at the back overlooked undulating meadows and woodlands, crowned by Mount Royal, on whose summit, amidst the thick foliage, gleamed the tall cross which in fulfilment of his vow Maisonneuve had himself borne up the steep mountain track. The house was a substantial building, long and low, with high peaked roof and overhanging eaves. The rooms were large, with low ceilings and immense chimneys taking up half one side of the wall. The furnishings bore evidence of wealth and comfort, displayed in old chairs and tabourets, their covers worked in satin stitch, the buffet and tables of cherry-wood all in plain solid bourgeois style. On either side of the street door were placed wooden benches, where the family and visitors gathered for recreation in the summer evenings. In a wing or annex adjoining was the shop, the foundation of the successful trader's wealth, in which were stored quantities of beaver-skins awaiting

43

shipment to France, as well as various commodities required by the settlers, and such provisions as were considered necessary in fitting out the voyageurs for their long expeditions to the West and for purposes of trade with the Indian tribes. At the back of the house the garden bloomed with fragrant, old-fashioned flowers ; there, too, carefully cultivated pear and plum trees revived a memory of Old France.

Though Le Ber's own family consisted of but a daughter and three sons, the household was a large one. His home was a capacious abode, extending a kindly welcome to all who might care to seek its shelter. And it was always full to overflowing ; friends, relatives, guests, servants and retainers thronged the roomy chambers. As at the settlement, its occupants were divided into two clearly defined parties who were always at daggers drawn—the worldly and the devout. In its earliest days Ville Marie had been regulated like a religious community. The mental atmosphere was saturated with hare-brained enthusiasm ; it was an age of miracles—the very existence of the little colony was a marvel. But the severity of the ecclesiastical rule and the unre-lenting vigilance of the Jesuits were resented by many of the more worldly spirits. In the midst of pressing dangers and heroic struggles there was a natural reaction in favor of the frivolous gaiety so character-istic of the volatile French temperament. The presence of a number of officers from France, too, whose piety was less conspicuous than their love of pleasure, served to keep this spirit of resistance alive.

The wealthy burgher's home had, owing to his daughter's renunciation of the world and its pleasures, acquired a peculiar sanctity in the eyes of his co-religionists. She, the richest heiress of New France, had in the bloom of her youth taken a vow of perpetual seclusion, poverty and chastity, in order to devote herself to a life of contemplation. The god-child of Chomody de Maisonneuve and Marguerite Bourgeois, brought up in an atmosphere of visions and miracles, the halo of saintship glittered before her young eyes like a diamond crown, and she entertained a firm determination to scale the steepest heights of virtue and self-sacrifice. Looking down with spiritual pride upon the common herd of Christians, busied with the ordinary duties of life, she eschewed the visible and present, aspiring only to live for the heaven beyond. Lost in the vagaries of an absorbing mysticism, Jeanne Le Ber was unrelenting in the practice of humiliation and self-abnegation. Wonderful stories of her superior sanctity were whispered abroad. She wore a horse-hair skirt and belt, allowed herself scarcely any sleep, and confined her diet to the coarsest and meanest of food. She held no communication with those nearest to her by ties of blood. Two years after her retirement from the world her mother was attacked by fatal illness, and though the sound of the poor woman's groans penetrated to her daughter's chamber, the would-be saint denied herself the privilege of attending her parent's death-bed. Though Jeanne Le Ber's face was never seen except by the one person who waited upon her, nor her voice ever heard by those most closely connected with her, yet from the secluded chamber which for several years she had never quitted, that voiceless presence exercised a potent ascendency.

This influence had operated most powerfully upon her brother Pierre, a youth of mystical tendencies. Sensitive, full of refinement, quick and impatient as a thoroughbred, he had been one of Charon's early associates—the only one who remained faithful to the end. Possessing keen artistic perceptions, he yet lacked power of execution. Few in the colony had either leisure or inclination for the cultivation of the fine arts, and Pierre Le Ber's paintings were received by his contemporaries with an admiration untinged by criticism. His early training had predisposed him to aceticism, but his natural temperament, against which he battled with ceaseless resistance, inclined him to a sensuous delight in beauty, harmony, and brightness. His religion was that of the affections and sentiments; his imagination, warmed by the ardor of his faith, shaped the ideal forms of his worship into visible realities. He displayed a curious ingenuity in inventing torments for himself, wearing a belt covered with sharp points, whipping himself with a scourge of small cords until his shoulders were one great wound, playing at beggar, eating mouldy food, and performing the most repulsive and disagreeable offices in hospitals. More than once the rich merchant's eldest son had been seen staggering through St. Paul Street with a lame beggar, whom he was bearing through the mud, seated on his back. As Jacques Le Ber de Senneville, the second son, was a man of the world of fashion and of courts, and Jean Le Ber du Chesne a man of action and energy, so Pierre was a dreamer of dreams, a beholder of visions.

The relations between Le Ber and the Marquise de Monesthrol had at one time furnished gossip to the small community at Ville Marie, which, during the long winter months cut off from the world, had little but scandal to serve as a diversion. On his return from a voyage to France the merchant was accompanied by the Marquise (a perfect type of the *grande dame* of the period), a child two years old, and a young attendant. Even to his closest friends Le Ber had never offered further explanation than to say that in his youth he had been under obligations to Madame de Monesthrol's family, and that on his return to France, finding her widowed and in trouble, he had been proud to offer her a home for herself and her orphan niece in the New World. The lady on her part always warmly acknowledged her indebtedness to the Canadian merchant. People coming out from France brought rumors of great pecuniary trouble which had fallen upon Madame's branch of the family, and of a terrible tragedy which had deprived her of her husband; but the most rampant curiosity sank abashed before the lady's dignified grace, while the maid Nanon's sharp tongue and ready wit were capable of repulsing all intrusive questions. Though Diane persisted in calling Le Ber her uncle, and in claiming his sons as cousins, it was plain that no tie of blood existed between them. The line of demarcation between patrician and plebeian was very clearly defined in those days ; no one could doubt the claim of the de Monesthrols to noble birth—indeed the family was one of the most noble and powerful of the kingdom of France—while Le Ber boasted of no pretension higher than the respectable *bourgeoisie*.

Nor was the obligation altogether on one side. It was whispered that even in her fallen fortunes the Marquise retained considerable influence at Court, that the appointment of Le Ber's second son as one of the Dauphin's pages, and later his commission in the Marines, had been due to her influence, and that the patent of nobility upon which the trader had set his heart would yet be obtained by the same favor. While anxious to obtain a high place for himself and his children in the heavenly kingdom, Le Ber's affections had by no means become alienated from the affairs of this world. It was conjectured by those who knew him best that a sincere reverence for rank was one of his prominent traits. As his daughter's aspirations after saintliness conferred upon him an especial distinction with the ecclesiastical authorities, so the Marquise's sojourn beneath his roof bestowed upon his home a stamp of fashion and exclusiveness to which he otherwise would have had no pretension. A patent of nobility had, some time before, been conferred upon his brother-in-law, Charles le Moyne, and it was bitter to the ambitious man that his own sons should be debarred from wearing the sword with which his nephews swaggered so gallantly.

Though born and bred in the focus of a most gorgeous civilization, reared like a princess amidst obsequious troops of vassals and retainers, having enjoyed a life of wit and splendor amidst a brilliant and dazzling society, and then suddenly, in her downfall, banished away to the ends of the earth, surrounded by perils and privations, Madame de Monesthrol wasted no time in vain regrets. Like many another of her class, she displayed a marvellous power of accommodating herself to circumstances and extracting pleasure and profit from them. In her former life she had loved, rejoiced and suffered with her whole heart ; now there was nothing for it but to make acquaintance with the practical and inexorable. She coolly counted chances and weighed consequences, and then, fully and freely, accepted the situation and its conditions. A submissive spirit might be patient, a strong will could supply resolution ; here existed an elastic mind, a willingness to seek comfort, a power of turning readily from evil to good, and of finding enjoyment in many simple occupations which carried her away from the memory of her sorrows.

In her fantastic French desire to act the new role to perfection she would fain have adapted herself more quickly than was possible to her new surroundings. She saw no reason why, with all the ease of a woman of the world and the loftiness of a great lady, she should not sell in the shop or undertake a share of the superintendence of the domestic affairs, as Le Ber's wife had done. She was promptly called from these delusions by Demoiselle* Le Ber's bewildered consternation, Nanon's shrill clamor, and more than all by the shocked and genuine distress of the trader himself.

"I am well aware, Madam la Marquise, that the home I have been able to offer is entirely unworthy your dignity. Have I failed in showing my appreciation of the honor your coming has conferred upon me that you should treat me thus?" the host reproached his guest.

"Even a dog can die," the lady replied with spirit. "I am not of puddle blood—I, Adrienne Monesthrol —that I should perish at the first breath of adversity. Still, my old and good friend, to whom I owe so much "—Madame laid her white jewelled hand upon the merchant's arm, and when she softened there was something wonderfully winning in this woman's proud gentleness—"if it pleases you best that I should remain seated like an image I must even yield, and give up all hope of being useful."

---

* Only ladies of rank were styled Madame.

Then Le Ber kissed the gracious hand respectfully, for by him the French lady was encircled with a halo of reverence.

Perceiving that her well-intentioned efforts had failed, Madame, philosophically reviewing all the facts of the case, graciously permitted herself to remain upon the pedestal where the loyalty of her devoted friend had placed her.

In New France the appendages of an old-established civilization flourished side by side with the rough usages of an almost unbroken wilderness. Amidst the solid comforts of this bourgeois home, the Marquise established a little court over which she reigned by sheer majesty, ruling without effort or design, governing because it was her nature so to do.

Madame's bedroom, which was the great chamber of reception, was always warm and heavily perfumed. In the upper part the bed was placed, raised above the rest of the room by a few steps, and further divided from it by a row of slight low pillars. The bed was an immense four-poster, seven feet each way, with gauze and silk curtains, and a blue satin counterpane embroidered with convolvulus and carnations. The space beside the bed, called the *ruelle*, was furnished sumptuously with pictures, statuettes, vases, gilded mirrors, fancy tables of buhl and ormolu, chairs and stools of various kinds covered with satin and destined to accommodate Madame's guests with wise adaptation to the rank and pretensions of each.

Before the window on a stand were pots of flowers,

and in small tubs bloomed orange trees, above which hung canaries in gilt cages. There were strips of Persian carpets on the floor ; mirrors gleamed in filigree frames ; a harpsichord stood in the corner. The chairs were of gilt ebony with cushions in tambour. Opposite Madame's chair hung the portrait of a young man, in lace cravat and half armor, the *cordon bleu* of the Order of St. Louis worn conspicuously across his velvet coat. The face was gay, reckless, handsome ; and before the picture hung a veil of silken gauze. Most people supposed this to be the portrait of the Marquise's husband ; Diane knew that it was that of the Marquis' younger brother, her own father, the Chevalier Raoul Anatole de Monesthrol, who had been killed while fighting with the King's armies in Flanders. On the 12th of May every year the Marquise spent the day in fasting and prayer. Though the subject was never alluded to, nor explanations ever offered, the young girl understood that this custom was in some way connected with her father's death.

A draped recess held an ivory crucifix and a Book of Hours. A trailing ruby velvet curtain veiled the door. A quaint sensuous charm hung about the apartment, which was enhanced by the stately figure of the lady herself. Like others of her station, Madame, however heavy at heart, was consummate mistress of her outward behavior. She sat with fan hanging on one arm and jewelled snuff-box within reach, her mobile aristocratic features displayed to advantage by her dress, a panniered robe of blue and silver brocade. Madame's common employment consisted in unpicking gold lace, which Le Ber disposed of for her in the regular market as bullion.

CHAPTER VI

MADAME'S "APARTEMENT."

EVERY evening, when Le Ber was at home, he
went up to kiss Madame's hand, inquire how
she did, or to play cards with her until the supper was
served at seven. Madame was gracious, with a sense
of supremacy and privilege; many a lesson in worldly
wisdom, too, the shrewd trader received from the
witty and sagacious woman of the world. Le Ber
had been brought up on the estate of the Marquise's
father, and the two, though so strangely dissimilar,
had many points of interest in common.

The Marquise de Monesthrol was partial to receptions in bed. On such occasions she wore a white
satin jacket, white gloves, a cornette or morning cap
of exquisite lace, and had the card-table so placed
that she could join in the game without awkwardness.
The visitors received greetings in tone apparently
easy and natural, yet in reality framed and graduated
with the most exquisite tact. In this Madame
resembled the great lady who enjoyed the reputation
of being so thoroughly well-bred that one could tell
merely from her pronunciation of the word "Mon-
seigneur" whether she were speaking to a Prince of

the blood, an ecclesiastical dignitary, or a peer of France.

Madame also enjoyed her evening "*apartement*," commencing at seven and ending at ten, whither her guests gathered to play lasquenet, hombre and brélan, while in the intervals between the deals Jean handed around frothed chocolate and muscat on a massive silver tray chased with armorial bearings. These receptions were a centre of wit—a wit delicate and subtle, but always natural and agreeable; they brought with them a reminiscence of the dazzling days of the lady's youth. Most of the party gathered there had passed through manifold troubles. In many cases it was misfortune which had driven them to quit their native land; disease, famine and death now stared them constantly in the face, yet they were proud and high-hearted, presenting an indomitable front to adversity. The common people might bewail their troubles—that was the privilege of their low estate— but whatever the dire necessity, the pressing emergency of the moment, it would have been deemed the height of ill-breeding for any of the Marquise's coterie to allude to any subject not capable of amusing and interesting the entire company.

It was a punctilious French circle, polished and occasionally extremely brilliant, in which refined artifice and trained coquetry were constantly exhibited; where a leader cleverly conducted the conversation and each individual present was under an obligation to contribute his or her share to the general entertainment. The men stood deferentially behind the high-backed chairs, treating skilfully the topics which the women had touched with dexterous grace. The conversation was cynical and epigrammatic, but always amusing. The Marquise was herself an accomplished talker. The light sarcastic humor, subtle touches, unsparing irony or ridicule—always kept within conventional bounds—with which her conversation flashed and sparkled, permeated the little circle and charmed all.

When she permitted her thoughts to dwell upon the subject (which was but seldom, for in her philosophic fortitude Madame objected to idle repinings), the Marquise thought that she had died when she left France—died to hope, and love and ambition,—and in this new world had revived again a sort of ghost of her former self to confront another existence. She could not dwell forever amidst the crumbling ruins of her life ; an entirely new array of troubles and difficulties had to be met, which nevertheless had a novel side, and took her mind from her own wounds. It might be painful to flesh and blood, but the cup had to be drained. The climax and agony of her youth had been left behind ; it still remained to tread with calmness the dark paths that stretched before her. In that case it was well to make endurance as pleasant as possible, to accept every solace and alleviation.

The Marquise represented the sceptical, worldly element in the household. While Le Ber's bourgeois tastes and habits prevented him from feeling much sympathy with those of his noble guests, he greatly prided himself upon Madame's social supremacy. He had no paltry vanity to obscure his clear perceptions, and his unquestioned autocracy was mellowed by a fine instinct of kindly courtesy. There were others more narrow-minded and less tolerant, but their ill-natured comments were ignored by the great lady. She held it becoming in a woman of quality not to fail in religious observances, but it was her nature to inspect everything curiously, to fathom intentions and analyze motives, and then to form her own judgments. Her enemies hinted that the Marquise had been infected by the Jansenist doctrines and that she had Jansenist books in her possession. She listened to all that was said, smiled suavely, but never altered her intention of not allowing her actions to be regulated by the narrow dogmas of the Jesuits. She still enjoyed her quiet game of piquet with Père Denys, a kindly and amusing man with a keen sense of humor, read the books which suited her, and exercised a charitable tolerance unknown to the fanatics by whom she was surrounded.

Diane was the heaviest weight upon Madame's heart. For herself she had done with all things, made the sacrifice of all things, but the child was young, all life lay before her. Had the demoiselle de Monesthrol remained in France she might have been received among the *dames nièces* of Remiremont, that refuge for penniless young girls of high lineage ; but in the colony, with all the outlooks of life uncertain, who could predict what the fate of a dowerless damsel might be? As Madame's opinion of colonial education was not high, she resolutely refused to send her niece to the Ursulines at Quebec, thus again scandalizing the clerical authorities.

"Would I see Diane a child of the pavement? a goat-herd—a little peasant? *Seigneur dieu!* what a horror! The loss of fortune may previously have afflicted us, but greatly as that is to be deplored, what is it to the lack of breeding?"

Madame de Monesthrol imparted to her niece the graces and accomplishments of which she was herself mistress, while Nanon took pride in instructing a quick if somewhat volatile and mischievous pupil in many useful domestic arts. The result was a broader culture, a wider range of sympathy, than could well have been gained in the seclusion of a convent. Climatic influences and the peculiar condition of colonial life had modified, not indeed the French lady's ideas of education, but the results derived from her system. In the hardy adventurous condition of New France, with every faculty called into play, and a constant demand on every energy, it was quite impossible that even a young girl of noble birth should retain the utter ignorance of the world, the absence of self-assertion, supposed to characterize the traditional French *jeune personne.* Madame watched this development with interest, curiosity, and some

amazement, but always remained strictly and philosophically impartial.

"I answer to you for it, Nanon, it was not so in my
time," she explained to her faithful attendant, who
was the only person to whom the lady ever really
extended her confidence. "I was timid and sensitive.
I scarcely dared raise my eyes when M. le Marquis
de Monesthrol was presented as my *futur*, the day I
left the convent. Diane knows no fear."

"Yes, Madame la Marquise, and we have all seen
the evil that comes of that sort of thing," was the
daring comment ventured by the waiting-maid; "let
our demoiselle have a chance for happiness in another
way." For an instant the Marquise's face looked wan
and haggard, but she quickly recovered herself.

"Happiness—where is it?" she mocked. "But for
the little one's fortune—I cannot make it, I must not
mar. Misfortune has fallen upon our generation;
Diane may be favored with a happier lot."

"Our demoiselle is of the best; noble and brave
and generous to the core," asserted Nanon confidently.

Very early marriages were the rule in the colony,
yet at eighteen Diane de Monesthrol, the fairest girl
in New France, still remained unwed. The demoiselle
Fresnoy Carion, her youthful companion and Le
Ber's ward, who had married Le Moyne de St. Helène,
at the same age was already a staid matron, the
proud mother of two curly-headed little ones. Many

matches had been proposed, but the girl seemed to be capricious and always raised objections, and Le Ber was invariably won over to support her side of the question. Had Madame in any case really exerted her authority opposition would have been useless, but some subtle intuition born of her own tragic experience caused her to refrain from doing so.

"I am perhaps not doing my duty by the child in not settling the affair at once," Madame ventured to say to her protector. "Should an occasion entirely favorable arise I should undoubtedly do so. Who is there to marry here but priests, partridges and wild turkeys? Say, is it not so, my friend?"

Le Ber gravely agreed to the Marquise's assertion. His ambitions were guided by so clear a sagacity that he rarely was forced to recede from a position once taken. He had his own ideas on the subject, which he kept strictly to himself. There was no hurry to seek an establishment for Diane de Monesthrol. His daughter and his eldest son were striving to establish themselves amidst the highest ranks of the heavenly aristocracy; it should be right to obtain for his younger sons similar worldly advantages. To what might not du Chesne aspire were his claims to consideration strengthened by an alliance with the noble family of de Monesthrol, who still possessed powerful connections in France? If no more advantageous offer presented itself Madame might in time be induced to overlook the presumption of his proposal; she was above all things eminently reasonable. It would be impossible to leave the girl alone in the world exposed to the buffets of fate. He would wait patiently for the realization of his plans.

Anne Barroy, a cousin and poor relative of Le Ber's, who acted as attendant to the recluse and was the only one who ever came into personal contact with Jeanne Le Ber, headed the priestly faction in the house. Anne was an exaggerated example of the extreme opinions that obtained in Ville Marie at that date. She had a stealthy way of moving about, with eyes cast down and hands folded meekly in front of her, as with pious ostentation she groaned aves and paters. Nanon boldly declared that Mam'selle Anne had eyes in the back of her head, and a nose long enough to reach the utmost limits of everybody's business. This good woman entertained profound convictions of the worthlessness and wickedness of the world in general ; she also deeply disapproved of the Marquise and her niece, and evinced a principle of active antagonism to Nanon, whose powers of sharp retort, audacity, and sauciness rendered her a formidable adversary. Her mind was forever dwelling upon their iniquities.

" They revel with fontanges and panniers, coquetry and late suppers," she lamented, " forgetful of the promises of their baptism ; like the unhappy Pretexta spoken of by our holy Bishop, who had her hands suddenly withered and who died five months afterwards, and was precipitated into hell because by order of her husband she curled the hair of her niece after a worldly fashion."

In reality Anne Barroy was a dull, narrow-minded woman, desperately loyal to her convictions, yet with sufficient cunning to know that her own claims to distinction rested upon the pretensions of her charge to superior sanctity ; and these she determined to uphold at all costs.

"They feast, those sinners, while that angel eats only the food left by the servants, and that, too, after it has become mouldy. She suffers from cold and hears the mass with arms outstretched in the form of a cross. What her reward will be we all know. Their punishment I leave in the hands of God and the saints."

A young Frenchman of noble family, who had been sent out to Canada by his relations on a *lettre de cachet*, was also a member of Jacques Le Ber's household. Louis de Thevet, Sieur d'Ordieux, had lost his father and was in hopes of succeeding him as *Lieutenant-Général des Eaux et des Forêts*, of the Duchy of Valois, an hereditary office in the family. His uncle and step-brothers induced him to sell it, promising that the Duke de Gusore would give him a lieutenancy in the infantry. The prospect failing him, he was afterwards sent to Canada, where he was left by his relatives entirely without resources. An effort had been made to send him to Louisiana, but he resolutely refused to serve as a private soldier, because, as he maintained, he was of noble birth.

Backed by Le Ber's powerful influence, he had contrived so far successfully to elude all efforts to dispose of him contrary to his own inclinations.

"The youth has great expectations; nor can his uncle be expected to live forever. He may yet be a great noble, powerful at Court. Those who befriend him will lose nothing," decided Le Ber.

CHAPTER VII.

A FOREST ADVENTURE.

THE Canadians, reduced to the last extremity by the vacillating policy of the late Governor, Denonville, had found in the Count de Frontenac a chief whom they could trust. Frontenac, realizing that prompt and bold action was necessary to sustain this confidence, resolved to take the initiative, and revive the prestige of the French arms by striking swift blows. The wandering Iroquois appeared as evasive as ghosts; but the English remained open to attack. Rumors began to circulate through the settlement that a war party was about to be organized. It was noticed that arms and provisions were being quietly collected. The women became anxious. The older men discussed the question gravely; the younger were wildly excited at the prospect of fighting.

Soon it became known that three bands of picked men were to start from Ville Marie, Three Rivers and Quebec, respectively; the first to strike at Albany, the second at the border settlements of New Hampshire, and the third at those of Maine. The party from Ville Marie was ready first. It consisted of two hundred and ten men, of whom ninety-six were Christian Iroquois from the two mission villages of Sault St. Louis and the Mountain of Ville Marie.

The French were mostly coureurs de bois. These restless spirits had shared in the general demoralization, and under Denonville's rule had proved unmanageable. Their chief virtues were hardihood and skill in woodcraft ; their principal faults insubordination and lawlessness. Tact and address were needed in guiding them. The leaders of the present expedition, thoroughly trained in the roving and adventurous character of Indian warfare, enjoyed the entire confidence of the hardy bushrangers. Le Moyne de St. Helène and d'Ailleboust de Mantet had the first command, supported by the brothers Le Moyne d'Iberville and Le Moyne de Bienville, with Repentigny de Montesson, Bonrepos, Le Ber du Chesne, and many other scions of the sturdy Canadian nobility.

There was difficulty in finding sufficient provisions for the expedition ; but finally, by seeking from house to house, getting here a few biscuits and there a flitch of bacon, enough was collected to supply a considerable party.

They began their march in the depth of winter. As they passed over the surface of the frozen St. Lawrence, each man had the hood of his blanket-coat drawn over his head and held a gun in his mittened hand ; a knife, a hatchet, a tobacco-pouch and a bag for holding bullets hung at his belt ; he bore a pack on his shoulders, while his pipe, in a leather case, was suspended at his neck. The blankets and provisions of the expedition were conveyed on Indian sledges.

Du Chesne was the gayest of the party, most of whom appeared to regard this adventure more as a frolic than a serious adventure. War was a pastime to these young Canadian seigniors, as well as the almost constant employment of their lives.

Crossing the forest to Chambly, they advanced up the frozen Richelieu towards Lake Champlain, for more than a century the great thoroughfare of war parties. The trees stood white as ghosts in the sheltered hollows of the woods, or shivered bare and gray on the wind-swept ridges. The Canadians made their way on snowshoes, with bodies half bent, struggling through frozen pine swamps, along deep ravines, and under frowning hill-sides. Their snowshoes broke on the hard crust or were shivered against rocks or the trunks of fallen trees. The woods resounded with jest and laughter as the gay bushrangers shouted at seeing one another catch and trip to sprawl awkwardly in the deep snow.

St. Helène, wishing to hold a council, ordered the company to halt. Frontenac had left the precise point of attack to the discretion of the Canadian leaders, who were familiar with all the conditions of the country through which they were passing, and the men had been kept in ignorance of their destination. The Indians had become distrustful, and now demanded to know where they were being taken. Fickle, wayward, and inconsequent as children, these allies must at the same time be conciliated and controlled, for it was impossible to do without their help. There always existed serious danger that they might repudiate the French alliance, join hands with the English traders, make peace with the Iroquois, and sacrifice their former friends without the slightest compunction.

"We are going to attack Albany," d'Ailleboust de Mantet said firmly. "We must reach that place or die in the attempt. We must obey the orders of our great father Onontio."

The Indians muttered angrily together. They declared the French had surrendered through cowardice the prisoners they had caught by treachery. The palefaces had expected their allies to bear the brunt of the war, and then left them to their fate. The Iroquois had actually burnt French captives in their towns.

"How long is it since the French have grown so bold?" shouted one in derision. "They have been shut up in their forts. Will they now fight in the light of day like men?"

"We shall fight or die," answered St. Hélène boldly. "Are our Indian allies squaws that they should fly at the first approach of danger? Before Onontio protected you you felt the teeth of the ravenous Iroquois dog. Our Governor tamed him and tied him up, but when Onontio was far away he devoured you worse than ever. We are strong enough to kill the English, destroy the Iroquois, and whip you if you fail in your duty to us. Will you let the English brandy that has killed you in your wigwams lure you into the kettles of the Iroquois?"

The Christian chief of Sault St. Louis, known as the "Great Mohawk," harangued his followers, exhorting them to wash out their wrongs in blood, but the savages remained turbulent, and seemed to be upon the point of deserting in a body. Their defection would mean the failure of the enterprise. At this juncture Le Ber du Chesne came to the rescue. Persuasion having failed he tried the effects of taunts.

"You are cowards!" he cried. "You do not know what war is; go back to your women and children. You never killed a man, and you never ate one except those that were given you tied hand and foot. Go home; we do not need your services."

Du Chesne gained his point. The pride of the warriors was aroused, and for the moment they were full of fight. The decision as to the point of attack was postponed, however, and the expedition moved on. When, after a march of eight days, they reached the Hudson, and found the place where two paths diverged, the one leading to Albany and the other to Schenectady, they took the latter. All agreed that an attack on Albany would be an act of desperation.

They bivouaced in the forest in squads of twelve or more. Digging away the snow in a circle, they covered the bare earth with a bed of spruce boughs, made a fire in the centre and gathered around it to smoke their pipes. Here crouched the Christian

savage muffled in his blanket, his unwashed face
bearing traces of the soot and vermilion he had
assumed for the war-dance in the square of the mission village. There sat the Canadian, hooded like a
Capuchin monk, but irrepressible in loquacity. The
camp-fire glowed on their bronzed and animated
features and lighted up the rocks and pines behind
them. The silent woods beyond presented a region
of enchanted romance and mystery.

Their slender store of provisions having been almost
all consumed or shared with the Indians, Le Ber du
Chesne was detailed to head a reconnoitring expedition of less than a score of men. Progress through
the snow-clogged woods was slow and painful ; the
lengthening days had brought a partial thaw, and the
little band waded through the melting snow and the
mingled ice, mud and water of the gloomy swamps.
Lowering gray clouds stretched monotonously over
the desolate waste. Their provisions soon exhausted,
they boiled moccasins for food, or scraped away the
snow to find hickory and beech nuts. Fires could not
be lighted lest the smoke should betray their presence.
Many suffered from frost-bites, and the men soon
were half dead with cold, fatigue and hunger.

The weather changed. Pelted by a cold, gusty
snowstorm, they lost the track and toiled on, shaking
down at every step a shower of fleecy white from the
burdened branches. It seemed impossible either to
advance or retreat. Thoroughly discouraged, shivering and famishing, it appeared as if nothing remained
but to lie down and die.

"I would that I could see the little home, or that I could at least have the blessing of a priest. It is ill to die like a rat in a hole," murmured le Canotier drowsily, as he sank down on the snow.

"Rouse thee, my fine big fellow!" shouted du Chesne. "Rouse thee if thou wouldst again see Ville Marie and Baboche and the little ones. I look to thee to show the spirit of a man, and to uphold the spirits of thy comrades."

"And what is this, mon Capitaine?" suddenly exclaimed le Canotier, starting up keenly alert, his hand instinctively grasping his knife.

Glancing over his shoulder du Chesne saw close beside him a plumed and painted Indian, standing motionless as a bronze statue.

"Adarahta comes to his French brother as a friend," muttered the Indian in guttural accents.

"And what would Adarahta?" demanded the young Canadian, his keen eyes striving to read the savage's expressionless features.

"Adarahta has been sent by the white chief to seek his young brother, who he feared was lost in the storm, to lead him to the spot where the French war-party camps."

"But you are not of our allies. You are an Iroquois," returned du Chesne, still distrustful.

"No, Adarahta is a son of the Great Mohawk. Taken captive by the Iroquois, treated as their slave, he would pay the debt he owes to his enemies. Is my French brother ready to follow?"

Still du Chesne hesitated. This might be some snare planned by the wily Indian to entrap them. Their circumstances were desperate, and this offer presented the possibility of escape. Action held a relief from hopeless suffering. It might be better to risk something than to perish miserably in the snow. The Canadians, feeble and emaciated, found it almost impossible to arouse themselves, but their leader addressed them in terms so animating that they caught his spirit and declared their readiness to push on.

" We follow," du Chesne decided. " Adarahta shall walk before me. At the first sign of treachery I shall shoot him like a wolf."

The Indian made no response. He moved silently in front, closely followed by the young commander, while the weary bushrangers dragged themselves through the drifts.

" Is the camp of our brothers far ? " asked du Chesne.

" Close at hand," responded the guide, as his eyes darted furtive glances in every direction.

" I would we were well out of this scrape. That painted fox means us ill," whispered le Canotier.

They had reached a narrow defile, the bed of a frozen stream, guarded on either side by high banks clothed with a labyrinth of bushes. Suddenly the air was filled with whoops and yells as scores of savages leaped from their hiding-places. As a rapid fire opened from the thickets, Adarahta fell beneath a death-blow from the leader of the expedition.

"Treachery! we are betrayed. Courage, my brave fellows!" shouted du Chesne. "Better to die fighting than to freeze in inaction. We shall sell our lives dearly."

So dense was the snow-storm that the Canadians could not well distinguish their advancing foes from those of their own party. The cries of the combatants were redoubled by the echoes of the narrow valley. In this moment of intense bewilderment the Canadians became broken and confused. Du Chesne ran to where the uproar was greatest, shouting, gesticulating, encouraging his men. Then he was suddenly plunged into a horror of thick darkness, and fell unconscious.

When Le Ber du Chesne recovered his hold on life he was lying in a wigwam attended by two squaws, who were awaiting the return of a party of Iroquois. The young Canadian alternately shivered and burned in the fever occasioned by his wounds. The Indian women were indifferently kind. They told him that he was to be carried to a distant Iroquois village; informing him also that the most of his party had been killed—only a few had managed to escape.

The young man's mind was still confused; fancy and reality blended inextricably together. Dreadful scenes of bloodshed, privation and misery mingled with memories of mirth and pastime. His thoughts travelled back to his home in Ville Marie. The father, stern and reticent, whose affection this youngest son had never doubted; the dead mother, whose tender care had been so sadly missed; the sister whose superior virtue he regarded with distant and respectful reverence—his heart turned to them with homesick yearning. Fancy dwelt most persistently upon the dear companion of his childhood, Diane de Monesthrol. He remembered her on her first arrival from France, a weary, dejected little stranger. Nanon's sharp tongue had been quick to remind the boy of the deference he owed to his father's noble guests, but the little French girl's affection had obliterated all class distinctions. What frolics and escapades they had had together! Diane had shown herself a trusty comrade, always ready to shield him, generously sharing with him every benefit. Far away in Ville Marie she would not forget to pray for him. This conviction brought comfort to his soul.

When he began to recover strength du Chesne's natural buoyancy of temperament soon reasserted itself. If he could become sufficiently strong to travel before his enemies returned he could easily make his escape. Each day his physical powers improved, and he had arranged all the details of flight when his hopes were abruptly crushed by the arrival of the Iroquois.

The Indians carried numerous scalps, and brought with them a number of prisoners. They vaunted their own exploits, and had no hesitation in proclaiming that there was nothing on earth so great as the Iroquois League. Being in haste to reach their own country they started at once, taking du Chesne with them.

73

The journey westward along the Mohawk valley was long and toilsome. They passed the first Mohawk town, Kughuawaga, standing on a hill, encircled by a strong palisade. Here the crowded dwellings of bark were shaped like the arched coverings of huge baggage waggons, and decorated with the tokens or armorial bearings of their owners. Gandagora was situated in a meadow. Tionondogue, the last and strongest of these fortified villages, stood, like the first, on a hill overlooking the river. On through the dense columns of primeval forest they marched, through swamps and brooks and gullies, until they emerged from the shadows of the woods into the broad light of an Indian clearing, where the town of the Oneidas stood. This place contained about one hundred bark dwellings, and numbered twice as many warriors.

Still advancing, they came at length to a vast open space where the rugged fields sloped upwards into a broad, low hill crowned with the lodges of Onondaga. In this capital of the Confederacy burned the council fires of five tribes. Here in time of need were gathered their wisest and best to debate questions of war and policy.

At a distance of some leagues they had been met by a crowd of the inhabitants, among them a troop of women bringing venison and corn, beaten together in a pulp and boiled, to regale the triumphant warriors. Here they halted and spent the night in songs of victory, mingled with the dismal chants of the prisoners, who were forced to dance for the entertainment of their captors. The next day, as they approached the town, the savage hive sent forth its swarms to meet them, and they were greeted with demonstrations of the wildest joy.

Du Chesne had visited many Indian villages. The bronzed groups gathered around the blazing fires, the flames of which painted each face in vivid light; the shrivelled squaws, grisly warriors scarred by many wounds, young braves whose honors were yet to be won, brown damsels flaunting in beads and ochre, the noisy children rollicking with restless dogs—all these were familiar sights to him. He was sufficiently intimate with their customs and prejudices to render himself agreeable. The adaptable young Canadian lost no opportunity of ingratiating himself. His good humor, gay songs, and clever mimicry afforded his hosts constant amusement. He knew these dusky denizens of the forest far too well, however, to suppose that his fate would be influenced by the favor in which he was held. In this focus of untrained savagery, ferocity was cultivated as a virtue, and every soft emotion was stifled as unworthy of a man. The son of the rich trader of Ville Marie, a youth who had already made a name for himself in the annals of Indian warfare, was far too rich a prize to be willingly relinquished. By words and signs he was constantly warned that his hour was come, and each day with renewed astonishment he found himself still among the living. Yet life contained many

chances; any moment might bring opportunity of
escape. So du Chesne betrayed no sign of trepida-
tion, but jested as merrily as though he were safe
within the precincts of Ville Marie.

It had been decided that the prisoners should be
distributed among the different towns of the Confederacy; only a young French lad named Gervais Bluet
remained with du Chesne. As a preliminary torment
an old chief tried to burn the captive's finger in the
bowl of his pipe. This was too much for the Canadian's philosophy, and without wasting words on the
matter he knocked his assailant down. A murmur of
approval arose from the spectators. If du Chesne
had begged for mercy their hearts would have been
hard as stone, but this proof of courage pleased the
warrior throng. He even contrived to make friends
among the savages, the most powerful of whom was
the famous Onondaga orator, Otréouate.

"If you destroy the wasp's nest you must crush the
wasps or they will sting you," declared the old man,
fixing his gaze reflectively on a great mask with teeth
and eyes of brass before which the Iroquois performed
their conjurations. "When our young men have
sung the war-song they will listen only to the sound
of their own fury. I would gladly save you, but it is
not in my power to do so."

"And what will be the manner of my death?" the
prisoner asked coolly.

"You will run the gauntlet. It has been decided
that the young white chief shall furnish entertainment

for the women and children. After that you will be devoured by fire."

"It is well," responded the young man quietly.

That day he gave his farewell feast, after the custom of those who know themselves to be at the point of death. When the company had gathered the condemned man addressed them in a clear voice :

"My brothers, I am about to die. Onontio's arm is long, and he will certainly avenge his children. That concerns you, not me. Do your worst ; you cannot make me shrink. I do not fear torture or death."

That night the white prisoners were closely watched. Two Indians slept one on either side of them, another being stretched across the door of the lodge. Du Chesne had formed no plan, he could depend upon no hope of reprieve, yet never did he entirely lose heart.

The next evening the captives were led out amidst the shouts of the women and children. The village was all alive with the bustle of preparation. The young white chief would furnish ample entertainment. The Iroquois formed themselves into long double lines, armed with clubs, thorny stocks, or slender iron rods bought from the Dutchmen on the Hudson. The prisoners were started to run between the two lines. They were saluted with yells and a tempest of blows. Bruised and lacerated from head to foot, and streaming with blood, young Bluet fell senseless to the ground. At the sight a sort of frenzy took possession of du Chesne. Seizing a club from one of the assailants, he used it with such vigor that his persecutors fell right and left beneath his blows. It was a valor born of sheer desperation, but it served him well. In their amazement the Iroquois became confused, and in the excitement du Chesne darted through an opening in the lines, and seeking shelter behind a wood-pile, found beneath it a hole into which he contrived to creep, and which afforded temporary concealment. A howl of furious consternation arose from the Indians. The prisoner had suddenly vanished. They ranged fields and forests in vain pursuit, and then concluded that their captive was a sorcerer who had been delivered by his Manitou.

From his place of hiding in the deepening darkness du Chesne could see much of what was going on around him. Once a tall savage passed so near that he could have touched him with his hand. The fate that awaited him if he were discovered, and the scarcely less terrible dangers of the wilderness that lay between him and his home, filled him with despair. Spent and exhausted he lay through the night in his cramped hiding-place, creeping out once to grope for a few ears of corn left from the last year's harvest. He wisely judged that his safety lay in remaining there till the savages out in search of him should return. So, though cramped and stiffened, he lay beneath the wood-pile till the following night; then when all was still, he slipped out, and had reached the outskirts of the village when, to his dismay, he stumbled over a log of wood. A sentinel immediately gave the alarm and the whole village started in furious pursuit. Du Chesne had been the fleetest runner among all his companions. He now had the advantage of a start and kept in advance of his pursuers, who took up the chase like hounds seeking game. When daylight came he showed himself from time to time to lure them on, then yelled defiance and distanced them again. At night all but two had given up the chase. Seeing a hollow tree, du Chesne crept into it, while the Iroquois, losing the trace in the dark, lay down to sleep near by. At midnight he emerged from his retreat, brained his enemies with a club, and continued his journey in triumph.

Du Chesne directed his course by the sun, and for food dug roots or peeled the soft inner bark off the trees ; sometimes he succeeded in catching tortoises in muddy brooks. He had the good fortune to find a hatchet in a deserted camp and with it made one of those wooden implements which the Indians used for kindling fire by friction. This saved him from his worst suffering, as he had but little covering and was at night exposed to tortures from cold. Building a fire in some deep nook of the forest he warmed himself, cooked the food he had found, and slept till daybreak, taking the precaution to throw water on the embers lest the rising smoke should attract attention. Through all hope beckoned him on. Life held so many prizes, offered so many delights, that at no time could he give way to despair.

Once he found himself near a band of Iroquois hunters, but he lay concealed, and they passed without perceiving him. Du Chesne followed their trail back, and found a bark canoe which they had hidden near the banks of the river. It was too large for his use, but he reduced it to convenient size, embarked and descended the stream. After that progress was comparatively easy. Finally, after enduring many hardships, he reached Ville Marie, where he was welcomed as one restored from the dead—the main expedition having, on returning from its successful attack on Schenectady, reported his capture by the Iroquois, from whom no mercy could be expected.

CHAPTER VIII.

VILLE MARIE.

BEAUTIFULLY situated as it was between Mount Royal and the St. Lawrence, at that early date Ville Marie could scarcely be termed imposing in appearance. It was busy and bustling, and had been described as "a place which makes so much noise, but is of so little account." A frontier town at the head of the colony, it was the natural resort of desperadoes of every description, offering a singular contrast between the rigor of its clerical seigniors and the riotous license of the wild crews which invaded it. Its citizens were mostly disbanded soldiers, traders and coureurs de bois—a turbulent population, whose control taxed to the utmost the patience, tact and ingenuity of the priestly governors. While a portion of the residents were given up to practices of mystical piety, others gambled, drank and stole; if hard pressed by justice they had only to cross the river and place themselves beyond seigniorial jurisdiction.

Limited as was the sphere of action, here existence offered many striking contrasts. In love with an exquisite ideal, men and women struggled to attain purity and unselfishness: they nursed the sick, fed

the hungry, loved and forgave, lived in godly fear
and died fortified by eternal hope; and this side by
side with those who yielded themselves up with bound-
less license to the worse passions of the human heart.

While scarcely more than a village in dimensions,
the preponderance of large buildings, churches and
convents imparted to the town a substantial appearance which the number of the population and its
scanty resources scarcely warranted. Quaint steeples
and turrets cut the misty pallor of the sky. Ville
Marie wore an aspect half military, half monastic. At
sunrise and sunset a squad of soldiers paraded in
front of the citadel; at night patrols marched through
the streets; church bells, deep and sweet mouthed,
rang out the Angelus morning, noon and night.

On the river-front were numerous taverns, in front
of which boats and canoes were drawn up on the
shore. Here voyageurs swaggered and swore, and
Indians, whom what Charlevoix quaintly terms "a
light tinge of Christianity" had scarcely redeemed
from savagery, squatted in sullen apathy or quarrelled
with brutal ferocity. A row of small compact
dwellings extended along a narrow street then, as
now, called St. Paul. Some of the houses were of
stone, but the majority were of wood with stone
gables, as required by law, the roofs covered with
shingles. All outlying houses were pierced with
loop-holes and fortified as well as the slender means
of their owners would permit. Gardens were mostly
fenced by pointed cedar stakes, with the poles firmly

tied together. Fields studded with scarred and blackened stumps stretched away to the bordering forest, crowding gloomy and silent on the right side and on the left. The green shaggy back of the Mountain towered over all.

Crowning the hill on the right stood the Seignior's windmill, built of rough stone, and pierced with loopholes to serve in time of need as a place of defence. This mill had a right to claim one-third of the grain brought to be ground; of which portion the miller received one-third as his share, and the Seminary required that the inhabitants should have all their corn ground there, or at one of the other mills owned by the priests.

Toward the left, on an artificial elevation, at an angle formed by the junction of a swift-glancing rivulet with the St. Lawrence, was a square-bastioned stone fort. This was the citadel of Ville Marie. About 1640, M. d'Ailleboust had removed the palisade of stakes which had formerly protected it, and had fortified it by two bastions. The fort was provided with artillery, and here, in command of a portion of the Carignan-Salière regiment, resided the military governor appointed by the Seminary.

Overlooking the river appeared the church of Notre Dame de Bonsecours, whose walls of rough grey stone have shone as a symbol of hope to the yearning eyes of many a weary voyageur, many a travel-worn emigrant. Above the entrance stood a statue of the Virgin, below which ran the inscription:

DIANE OF VILLE MARIE.

" Si l'amour de Marie
Dans ton cœur est gravé,
En passant ne l'oublie
De lui dire un avé."

The Hotel-Dieu, founded in 1644 by Madame de Bouillon, fronting on both St. Paul and St. Joseph (now St. Sulpice) streets, was an abode of much charity, tender devotion and heroic self-abnegation. The nuns, a devoted sisterhood, nobly conspicuous in the annals of the colony, excelled in acts of kindness which had become sacramental symbols of faithful obedience to God and loving brother-hood with man. Under their snow-white wimples beat hearts as brave as ever stirred under the robe of statesman or gorget of soldier. The church stood on St. Paul street, and was of stone in Tuscan style, sur-mounted by a triangular pediment and cross. The buildings consisted of hospital, convent and church.

On a gently swelling knoll west of the citadel stood the edifice erected by M. Charon as a hospital. Far-ther back, to the left, was the Jesuit church, fronting on Notre Dame street. Adjoining this was the College, a very small structure with large and care-fully cultivated gardens attached. The buildings of the Congregation of Notre Dame faced on St. Paul street, while the back windows overlooked the river; they were surrounded by a high stone wall. Here Marguerite Bourgeois, assisted by a band of noble women, labored for the conversion of the savages, and here the young girls of Ville Marie received all the instruction they were likely to obtain. Back of the settlement ran from the citadel a rough country road, which is now Notre Dame street.

Fronting the river on the line of the street were the enclosures and buildings of the Seminary, fortified, as was the Hotel-Dieu, to resist the attacks of the Iroquois. The ancient edifice was of the same shape as the present, forming three sides of a square, surrounded by spacious grounds. The priests' gardens were already renowned for the delicious quality of their fruit. The air of thrift and comfort which characterized the belongings of the clergy presented a painful contrast to the extreme penury of the colonists. With them, method, industry and frugality had resulted in abounding prosperity. The parish church of Notre Dame was directly in the centre of Notre Dame street. It was a low edifice, built of rough stone, pointed with mortar ; the high-pitched roof, covered with tin, reflecting the sunshine in dazzling brightness. The principal entrance was at the south end, and on the south-west corner was a tower, surmounted by a belfry. The public market was near the river, directly facing the Seminary property. This was a favorite rendezvous for all loiterers, as were also the the public wells, which, to suit the general convenience, had been placed near the Seminary, at the market-place, and in the Jesuits' garden. Here the citizens gathered. The women enjoyed the opportunities of gossiping at the well, their tongues moving as swiftly as the running water, their whole bodies aiding with an endless variety of appropriate gestures.

The men, with a vivacity that never diminished, held choleric arguments, or repeated marvellous stories. They tapped their foreheads, clasped their hands, clutched impetuously at perruques that presented a wonderful impunity from becoming disarranged. They discussed how Jean Louis had strained his right arm and fallen under the power of a sorcerer; how the good St. Anne had rescued Pierre Boulot and his comrade from shipwreck because they had made a vow in her honor; how Mère Bouillette had been tormented by the lutin in the shape of a will-o'-the-wisp, and the good Mère Berbier, of the Congregation of Notre Dame, had presented Madelon with a scapulaire as a charm against fever. It was whispered that it was feared that Georgeon and his fifty wolves, invisible when hunted by honest men, were driving the colts about at night. With bated breath they spoke of the dreaded scourge, the Iroquois, and then, with tears still glistening in their eyes, they broke into merry laughter at some careless jest. The rigor of the climate prevented much indulgence in that pleasant outdoor life in which the French peasant delights, but as soon as the late northern spring broke forth, and the air became soft and balmy, the natural instincts reasserted themselves.

To the east of the town, where Viger Square now stands, stretched a swampy marsh where the bulrushes

raised their tall heads and the stately purple iris
bloomed in profusion ; there the long-drawn plaintive
cry of the water-fowl echoed through the stillness in
melancholy cadences. Back of the settlement, par-
allel with Notre Dame street, a stream with mimic
rush and roar urged its way to the river. Between
this and the street, removed from the noise and bustle,
lay the quiet cemetery. Some distance away, to the
left, nestling at the foot of the mountain, was situated
the Mission village established by St. Sulpice for the
Christianized Indians. It was dominated by two
round stone towers, which afforded considerable protection to the colony ; a few French soldiers were
always stationed here. Near at hand, in winter half
buried in peaked drifts and massive banks of snow,
was the shrine of Notre Dame des Nièges.

Opposite the city, on the south bank of the St.
Lawrence, extending from Longueuil to Laprairie, lay
the fief acquired by that brave colonist Charles Le
Moyne, the brother-in-law of Jacques Le Ber. His
son, the Baron de Longueuil, notwithstanding the
conditions of painful change and fluctuation that attended the fortunes of the colony, reigned like a feudal
noble at Longueuil. His stone fort, flanked by four
strong towers, resembled a fortified French chateau.
A church and various substantial stone buildings clus-
tered around it. On St. Helen's lovely isle, rising
with gently wooded slopes out of the water, the troops
often camped. Opposite La Salle's Seigniory at La
Chine, on the south bank, was Sault St. Louis (Caugh-
nawaga), an Indian mission station.

Ville Marie was open to attack on all sides. The town had been recently fortified with palisades. The few defences it possessed were in very indifferent condition. The country around, and for nearly a hundred miles below it, was easily accessible to the Iroquois by the routes of Lake Champlain and the Upper St. Lawrence. In the unsettled and variable condition of the colony, the clerical influence maintained a certain solidity of aim to the community which they had originated, and in which they certainly were the ruling influence.

A Christian outpost established in the wilderness, ravaged by foes, feeble from the exhaustion of a starved and persecuted infancy, Ville Marie still contrived to exist.

Amid all the conflicting elements of her new surroundings, Lydia Longloy contrived dexterously to steer her way. In her old home she had been taught to regard the French as "bloodthirsty heathen," but with easy adaptability and admirable tact she now showed herself quite as ready to adopt the faith and opinions of these new friends as she was to follow their fashions and manners. A beguiling innocence was her chief characteristic, accompanied as it was by a soft amiability and teachableness both touching and flattering.

Père de Mereil, of the Seminary, who spoke the English language and devoted himself especially to the conversion of heretics, declared enthusiastically that this young girl was the most interesting convert he had ever been privileged to instruct. If the English captive were occasionally betrayed into frivolity by the levity of youth, the worthy priest ascribed these lapses entirely to the worldly influence of Mademoiselle de Monesthrol. Lydia had an easy way of explaining herself to be always in the right, and it would be unjust to attribute the pretty creature's innocent vanity and frank simplicity to other than natural childish frailty.

Heedlessly generous with the divine faith of youth, Diane de Monesthrol gave her love to the stranger. During the long illness which followed Lydia's removal to Ville Marie, Diane nursed her with tender care, and in her helplessness she had twined herself around the closest fibres of Diane's heart. She might not be either very strong or very wise, but she was her own pet, the joint protegè of herself and du Chesne. Lydia's trials and sufferings invested her with a halo of romantic interest. Diane's own glowing imagination conferred upon the Puritan maiden qualities of which the stranger had formed no conception. Her pure and simple beauty would have shone alike at a cottage door and in the halls of princes.

Lydia rejoiced in the sweet and exhilarating consciousness of an approving Providence. She found herself placed exactly to her taste. Dreading pain, she was only too well pleased to be allowed to forget the past ; finding herself flattered and caressed, she desired nothing better than to enjoy the present. An orphan, thrown upon the charity of distant and reluctant relatives, her life had not been happy. She had no enthusiasm, no imagination, no warm human sympathy to render the severe existence of her childhood endurable. Without in the least realizing it, Lydia had been bored to extinction. She hated now to think of those long, unlovely years of repression of her natural faculties. She had been accustomed to be looked down upon by her thrifty New England kindred, who had felt no hesitation in sharply chiding her shortcomings. There her beauty had been of small account ; she had no chance of wearing beautiful clothes, and had never listened to the sweet accents of flattery. Her various misdeeds had been severely visited upon her, her frailties exposed to open scorn, with the cheerful prospect held over her that in another existence these trifling vanities should be still more actively rued in fire and brimstone.

Thinking of all this Lydia Longloy rejoiced in her new freedom with the whole strength of her trivial soul. The Puritan settlement of Grotton, near Boston, with its memories of friends and neighbors, its precise restraint and rigid formality, became merely an unpleasant remembrance to be crushed out of sight. All the strict discipline of her New England training fell from her like a cast-off garment. She learned French with rapidity, absorbing the ideas and sentiments of those among whom her lot was cast.

She adopted powder and patches, fans and feathers, as though to the manner born. She acquired a deliciously arch imitation of the Marquise's airs; and if she missed Diane's dainty grace, her coquetry had a touch of sweet naturalness as of a child's affectation and extravagance. Once she found that to be pious was considered essential, thereafter her piety satisfied even Anne Barroy.

In the large, hospitable household one more or less made very little difference. Le Ber smiled indulgently upon what he considered his ward's new caprice, but for him the English prisoner had no charms. There were two whose favor she never succeeded in winning: these were Madame de Monesthrol and Nanon, who quickly arrived at a very distinct perception of the situation.

"Plebeian to the core," Madame nodded her stately head sagaciously, smelling at her *flacon* as if to keep off infection. "The little one waters a barren field. All that will count for nothing. This English girl will keep all she can get, and she is clever at getting. Yet one is young but once—can one blame her faith?"

Nanon was still more outspoken in her opinion.

"Bah! that crocodile blonde demoiselle. There are two words to a bargain, and our demoiselle will always be a loser, for she is of those who give lavishly with both hands; this other is a sponge who absorbs all and yields nothing in return."

CHAPTER IX.

AN OCCASION OF REJOICING.

THE existence of the colony depended upon the fur trade, and for nearly three years the Iroquois, with malicious ingenuity, had contrived to block up the main artery of commerce, the river Ottawa, thus stopping the flow of the country's life-blood. The annual supply of beaver-skins cut off, the settlement was compelled to exist upon credit. During the preceding winter the need had been so great that the authorities were obliged to distribute the soldiers among the inhabitants to be fed. Canada had been reduced to the last extremity, her merchants and farmers were dying of hunger. But relief was at hand.

One day, shortly before the annual fair, a messenger came in hot haste with the startling information that Lake St. Louis was covered with canoes. It must be an Iroquois invasion, and if so it was not an impossibility that the whole community might be destroyed. Cannon were fired to call in the troops from the detached posts, the churches were thronged by excited women and children, and the steady march of trained soldiers resounded through the streets. The authorities meanwhile were engaged in anxious consultation.

Suddenly alarm was changed into frantic joy by the arrival of a second scout, announcing that the new comers were not enemies but friends, who instead of destruction had come to bring good fortune to Ville Marie. Frontenac's courage and policy had at length succeeded in accomplishing the difficult but absolutely indispensable task of opening the Ottawa. Louvigny and Perrot, the envoys sent to the Indians by the Governor in the spring, whose persuasions had been supplemented by the news of the late victory gained on the Ottawa and the capture of Schenectady, had executed their mission satisfactorily. Despoiled of an English market for their furs, the savages were willing to seek sale for them among the French. Two hundred canoes had come laden with the coveted articles of merchandise which had for so long been accumulating at Michillimackinac.

It seemed as though good fortune, like ill-luck, were not to come alone. While three years of arrested sustenance came down from the great lakes of the West, a French fleet, freighted with soldiers and supplies, sailed up the St. Lawrence. This sight at any time was a reason for rejoicing. It meant news from home, succor from want, encouragement, relief. A moment had changed mourning apprehension into the ease and composure of perfect security. Almost dizzy with the sweetness of relief, struggling to retain sober consciousness, men cheered and laughed, while women who had worn a brave smile during the day of trouble now wept hysterically. As they looked into each other's eyes, the colonists realized how terrible had been the strain through which they had passed.

As they drew near, the savages, ever delighting in noise, fired their guns, while the deep continuous roar of cannon from the citadel greeted them as they landed before the town—woods, waves and hills resounding with the thunder of artillery. A great quantity of evergreen boughs was gathered for the use of the Indians, and of these they hastily constructed their wigwams outside the palisades. The Governor-General had come up from Quebec to meet the Indian allies. These negotiations, political and commercial, were of the utmost importance to the settlement ; there was scarcely an individual in all the colony who was not keenly interested both in the Council which was now to be held and in the great fair.

Moved by the universal impulse, Diane and Lydia, attended by Le Ber du Chesne, the Chevalier de Crisasi, and the Sieur d'Ordieux, started to attend the Council meeting. Nanon, thoroughly enjoying the occasion, walked behind. Nothing escaped the notice of her quick eyes or the comment of her unruly tongue.

" It is well said that good blood never lies. Our little partridge holds her own with the best ; those who have taste turn their heads to look at her. Well

they may ; a great lady is not a sight to be met with
every day in this part of the world, where every
trader's wife and daughter would like to perk their
heads with their betters. It is an *officier bleu*, no less,
or some great noble at the King's Court, who should
claim our demoiselle as his bride, and think himself
lucky to get her besides."

Diane's gown of heavy coffee-colored brocade had
a train which swayed gently behind, not dragging,
but caught up gracefully and drawn through both
pocket holes, displaying the laced skirt and the pretty
shoes on which jewelled buckles glittered. Her corsage was long waisted and close fitting ; clouds of
lace hung from the sleeves, while a lace fichu was
crossed over the bosom and fastened by some fragrant
crimson roses.

On either side of Mademoiselle de Monesthrol
walked the Chevalier and the Sieur d'Ordieux. The
first was a remarkably elegant and distinguished-
looking man. The thin dark face set within its
frame of powdered hair was somewhat languid and
supercilious ; the melancholy eyes were almost ori-
ental in their depth and intensity of expression.
The Marquis de Crisasi and his brother, the Chevalier, were Sicilian noblemen who had compromised
themselves by taking the part of France against
Spain. Their immense possessions were confiscated,
and, by a sudden turn of fortune's wheel they had
been precipitated from the highest pinnacle of prosperity down to bitter adversity. They had been

sent out to Canada in command of French troops.
The favor proved, in this case as in many others, a
most unreliable dependence. The Marquis had been
appointed Governor of Three Rivers, a poor post,
where it was almost impossible to keep from starving.
The Chevalier, who was regarded by his contemporaries as a model of every knightly virtue and accom-
plishment, neglected and forsaken by his friends at
the Court, waited for those marks of royal favor
which he was never to receive.

"For M. le Chevalier, his day is past," decided Le
Ber promptly ; "those who are cast off by the Court
have no future."

But the Chevalier was one of Madame de Monesthrol's warmest personal friends, valued by her for his
high breeding and personal worth.

The Sieur d'Ordieux was a little man who, in the
desire to increase his stature, used such high heels
that he seemed to be walking upon stilts. He wore a
long black wig, powdered and curled in front. He
was always decked in finery like a woman, steeped in
perfumes, glittering with jewelry and ornamented with
fluttering ribbons. This youth was a common type
of the men who strolled in the gardens of the
Tuilleries or in the galleries of Versailles, pulling the
strings which set the cardboard toys—the *pantins*—in
motion ; embroidering at women's frames in women's
salons ; gambling away body and soul at the receptions given by great Court ladies, or fighting bloody
duels at Longchamps on account of frail Court

beauties. Many of these men were driven by misfortune or their own reckless folly to the New World. When receiving their baptism of fire the high heads were dauntless and dignified ; these reckless triflers, when brought into contact with real conditions and necessities, proved themselves equal to the occasion— the most graceless young spendthrifts often showing themselves to be brave soldiers and gallant gentlemen.

Just now the Sieur d'Ordieux certainly could not be considered interesting. His conversation related exclusively to his own interests and exploits—the Court, the injuries and indignities which his relatives had inflicted upon him, the grandeur of his expectations. The Chevalier walked in dignified silence. His doleful glances inspired Diane with a teasing wish to coax and torment. She was young, thirsting for some deep emotion, moved by swaying currents of feeling of whose origin she had formed no conception. Consequently her smiles encouraged the loquacious youth, whose vanity never at any time required stimulant.

" *Misericord !*—but they are fools, these men," soliloquized Nanon, who appreciated the humor of the situation. " This little turkey believes that the world is created for him and his brood to strut and crow in. That poor, good, jealous Chevalier has grown as thin as a nail, and makes such sighs. He is furiously displeased, that one, and he never guesses it is for the grocer's son that our demoiselle plays the coquette.

Comment! but it is inconceivable that the Sieur du Chesne perceives nothing."

Du Chesne's handsome young face was shaded by a large musquetaire hat of felt in which a freshly curled white plume waved gaily. He wore a new crimson coat, bordered with a gold band in a fashion called at that time *à la bourgogue.* Black silk stockings displayed the perfect symmetry of his limbs. It was a costume not unworthy a young man's vanity. De Crisasi and d'Ordieux both wore swords which clanked at every step. The knowledge that his favorite son was without one cost Le Ber many a poignant pang.

Lydia walked demurely at du Chesne's side. Her fresh face, tinged with excited color, stood out in bewildering contrast to the flaxen hair. The neat dress of dark camlet with its snowy frills and "pinners," which had formed her Puritan costume, had been exchanged for an imitation of Diane's dress. Mademoiselle de Monesthrol delighted in decking out her protegé in the best she had ; nothing was too good to heighten the charm of the blonde beauty.

"This is likely to be an expensive whim," Madame had remarked to Le Ber. "It would have been better, my friend, to have provided Diane with the little negro boy of whom you have so often spoken. The imp would have been less mischievous than this colorless English girl."

Le Ber shook his head. Though a Frenchman he

was a man of few words. Many critical issues had been confided to his judgment with advantageous results. Was it possible that a frail, silly girl should have power to thwart the plans which he had labored with a refinement of elaboration to perfect?

As they neared the encampment Lydia gave a frightened start. "I dread the savages. The very glance of these painted monsters makes me faint and ill," she whispered nervously.

Diane paused with quick compunction.

"It is I who should have thought of that. You have nothing to fear, little one, with du Chesne at your side. Leave her not, even for an instant, my friend. Remember the terrible trial through which she has passed."

Lydia reddened to her very throat, and turning around flashed upon the young man such an odd, piteous, pleading glance that it startled him. Her naïveté was as novel as her beauty; every glance had a glamor of magic. She was attractive with that undefinable charm that belongs to some women, a magnetic quality not depending upon faultlessness of physical beauty. A very child, she carried herself with an air of innocently transparent indifference, with her ready blushes and her pettish, winning face. She was so petulant that du Chesne was amused, and found his charge extremely interesting. When, some time later, Diane, finding herself at his side, whispered words of thanks for his consideration, he shook his head in protest, laughing in a startled, gratified sort of way ; then turned from the subject with the careless ease which was one of his characteristics.

"It is to you she owes her life. I want you really to like her, du Chesne," the girl pleaded warmly.

"It would not be difficult to do that!" and du Chesne laughed again.

CHAPTER X.

THE COUNCIL.

A LARGE oblong space was marked out on a common between St. Paul street and the river, and enclosed by a fence of branches. In this enclosure the Council upon which such momentous issues depended was held. Some of the Indians who attended had gathered from a distance of fully two thousand miles. The assembly presented a strange and grotesque appearance. There were Hurons and Ottawas from Michillimackinac; Pottawatomies from Lake Michigan; Ojibways from Lake Superior; Crees from the remote north; Mascoutins, Sacs, Foxes, Winnebagoes and Menominies from Wisconsin; Miamis from St. Joseph; Illinois from River Illinois; Abenakis from Acadia, and many allied tribes of less account. These sang, whooped and harangued in their several accents. Their features were different; so were their manners, their weapons, their decorations, their dances. Each savage was painted in diverse hues and patterns, and each appeared in his dress of ceremony—leather shirt fringed with scalp-locks, colored blanket, robe of bison-hide or beaver-skin, bristling crest of hair or long lank tresses, eagle feathers or skins of beasts. A young

Algonquin warrior, in the dress of a Canadian, was crowned with drooping scarlet feathers and a tall ridge of hair like a cock's crest. A chief of the Foxes, whose face was painted red, wore an elaborate French wig, the abundant curls of which were in a state of complete entanglement. He persisted in bowing right and left with great affability, lifting his wig like a hat to show that he was perfect in French politeness.

The Indians, feathered, greased and painted, were seated in close ranks on the grass, braves, chiefs and sachems gravely smoking their pipes in silence. Troops, making the best possible show, were drawn up in lines along the sides. At one side, under a canopy of boughs and leaves, were seats for the spectators; these were occupied by ladies, officials, and the principal citizens of Ville Marie. In front was placed a chair for the Governor-General.

The French yielded themselves up readily to the spirit of the occasion. The whole community had recently passed through unheard-of sufferings, yet on the appearance of the faintest gleam of sunshine the colonists were ready to smile, to deck themselves out in their bravest, to seize eagerly all the brightness of the hour. Eyes and jewels flashed, brocades rustled, feathers waved, and here and there was a shimmer of filmy lace. In carf and coif, ladies whose noble manners, stately bearing and sparkling wit would have fitly graced the Court of Versailles, whose elegant and ingenious coquetries were the product of the most finished civilization, promenaded, escorted by officers bedecked with gold and silver lace and all the martial foppery rendered necessary by the etiquette of the day.

"Vive M. le Comte de Frontenac! It is M. le Gouverneur who has saved us from the clutches of those vultures, the Iroquois! Yes, and opened the fur trade, that we may not starve! Vive le Gouverneur!" shouted the crowd.

Frontenac's gallantry and open-handed liberality, his success in dealing with the Indians, the prosperity which his policy had brought to Canada, rendered him the idol of the populace, who had not been blinded by jealousy or rent by internal divisions, as were the officials, civil, military and ecclesiastical, all of whom apparently wanted to obtain aid from the Government. In the upper classes every man had a grievance against somebody or something, of which he was continually writing complaints to France. These bickerings and animosities added, at least, a spice of variety to the life of the colony.

A detachment of guards in the King's livery preceded the Governor, who was surrounded by a brilliant retinue of young nobles, gorgeous in lace and ribbons. Louis de Buade, Comte de Frontenac, Chevalier de l'Ordre de St. Louis and Governor-General of New France, had already attained his seventieth year, though the alert, decided movements of the bold and impetuous soldier showed no diminution of vitality. He represented the best type of

French courtier and gentleman soldier of the reign of
le Grand Monarque. A fine martial figure, erect and
vigorous, the natural distinction of his mien and pose,
the assured ease of look and manner, marked him as
one familiar with the usages of courts. His keen
black eyes shone beneath a broad brow upon which
the years, with their many troubles, had traced
scarcely a wrinkle. The Roman nose, thin lips, and
firm, prominent chin, imparted a severe and imperious
expression to his face. He wore a wig, lightly powdered, with long ringlets falling on either side of his
face, crowned by a three-cornered hat bordered with
gold. His fine red surtout and short embroidered
vest were of the latest fashion ; his loosely knotted
cravat was of point lace, while his white and delicate
hands were partly concealed by falling ruffles of the
same. He wore shoulder and sword knots. A broad
belt, inlaid with gold, fell from his right shoulder,
encircling the waist, and held a sword whose hilt,
resting upon the left hip, glittered with jewels. His
shapely limbs showed to advantage in long black silk
stockings and shoes with jewelled buckles. The Governor had a decided taste for splendor and profusion,
delighting in brilliancy of clothing and luxury of
service. All his surroundings presented as much
pomp and magnificence as the slender resources of
the colony would permit. This was an hour of
triumph precious to the daring and potent spirit of
the French noble, who fully perceived the force of his
own position. Some time before he had been recalled

in disgrace owing to the machinations of his enemies, and during his absence the colony's fortunes had fallen to their very lowest ebb ; he had now returned to taste the sweetness of success, and even his foes were forced to acknowledge the beneficial results which his policy had already achieved.

Near the Governor stood the interpreters, whose services where constantly required, while scattered about were a number of Canadian officers nearly every man of whom had been the hero of some marvellous exploit. Here was the Chevalier de Callière, Governor of Ville Marie, dark and haughty, almost as imperious as Frontenac himself, a man respected by the savages and adored by his own men. His rival, de Vaudreuil, a fluent, voluble Gascon, was in attendance upon the beautiful Louise de Joybert of Quebec, who was soon to become his bride, and had little attention to give to the animated conversation of d'Ailleboust de Mousseaux, Civil and Criminal Magistrate of Ville Marie, and his brother d'Ailleboust de Mantet, who had won laurels at the taking of Schenectady. All three courteously saluted Boisberthelot de Becancourt and Augustin le Gardeur de Coutremanche as they passed. Leaning on his sword stood the Sieur d'Hertel, who at the head of fifty Canadians and savages had taken Salmon Falls during the winter of 1690. Near by, Boucher de Boucherville, who with forty-six Frenchmen had held the fort of Three Rivers against five hundred Iroquois, was holding animated discussion with the Sieur de

Montigny, whose body bore traces of conflict in innumerable wounds, and who in command of only twelve Canadians had taken forcible possession of Portugal Cove, and with M. de Pontneuf, son of the Baron de Becancourt, the preceding winter had gallantly silenced the eight cannon defending Casco. On one side the Sieurs de Beaujeu, de St. Ours, Baby de Rainville, de Lanandière, Deschambault, Chartier de Lobiniére, d'Estimanville, de la Brossee, Repentigny de Montesson, Captains Subercase, d'Orvilliers, Sieur de Valrennes, and his lieutenant, M. Dupuy, conversed with something emphatically Gallic in their vivacious gestures and absorbed faces.

The clergy were also well represented. Talking to the Marquise de Monesthrol appeared Dollier de Casson, Superior of the Seminary, gigantic in stature, hearty of voice, with bold, brown, earnest face, frank and simple in expression. He had been a cavalry officer, and had fought bravely under Turenne; the soldier and the gentleman still lived under the priest's hassock. Father Joseph Denys, Superior of the Recollets, benign and jovial, basking openly in the Governor's favor, eyed jealously askance by the Jesuits, stood close behind Frontenac. Father Denys had to a great extent shared the Governor-General's disgrace; the period of Frontenac's banishment had proved evil days for the Recollets, and their Superior would have been more than human had he not exulted in their present exaltation.

In a group apart stood Jacques Le Ber, Le Moyne

de Longueuil, La Chesnaye, de Niverville and Aubert de Gaspé. Some of these men had been the Governor's most resolute antagonists during his first term of office, and were not at all sure of the ground upon which they were treading or the turn which affairs were likely to take.

Now ensued a striking scene, an essential preliminary to the treaty which the Governor-General hoped to conclude with the Indians. Few white men have ever surpassed the Count in skill in dealing with the aborigines. Those who had succeeded to his position after his recall to France had utterly failed in this direction. The only hope of maintaining this little settlement planted in the wilderness was in inducing the other Indian tribes to unite in a determined resistance to the encroachments of the Iroquois. He now listened to their orators with gravest attention, as though weighing every word that was uttered. When, in his turn, he addressed them with an air of mingled kindness, firmness and condescension that inspired them with respect, their expressions of approval came at every pause in his address. Then with the same ceremonious grace with which he might have bowed before Louis the Magnificent, the Governor grasped the hatchet brandished it skilfully in the air, and in a clear, strong voice, intoned the war-song. To a punctilious courtier the position might have seemed utterly absurd, but Frontenac was a man of the world in the widest sense, and as much at home in a wigwam as in the halls of princes; as a diplomat he retained a clear, logical perception of all the facts of the situation. Many, under such circumstances, would have lost respect by an undignified performance, but the Count's native tact enabled him to harmonize the most incongruous elements; the faculty of imitativeness, the utter absence of self-consciousness, the determination faithfully to execute a disagreeable duty, served his purpose. Instead of exciting ridicule his achievements delighted the Indians, aroused his friends to enthusiasm, and extorted a reluctant admiration even from the most determined of his opponents.

"This poor M. le Gouverneur! he possesses my sincere sympathy. Figure to yourself how these cries and howls, worse indeed than those made by the wild beasts of the forest, must prove trying to the throat," remarked the Marquise, with a sincere appreciation of the loyalty involved in undergoing so very objectionable an ordeal.

The principal officers present followed the example of their chief; indeed, not a little ambition was shown as to who should go through the ceremony with the most perfect accuracy, and some of the younger members of the party, who had become familiar with forest life, displayed much agility and derived apparent enjoyment from the ceremony.

At first the savages stood stolid, silent, making no response to the invitation extended to them. It was an interval of anxious suspense. Suddenly the

Christian Iroquois of the two neighboring missions
rose and joined the Frenchmen ; then, as though im-
pelled by some irresistible impulse, the Hurons and
Algonquins of Lake Nipissing did the same. One
wild tribe after another followed this example, until
the whole troop joined in the stamping and screeching
like an army of madmen, and the Governor with
grave dignity led the dance, stamping and whooping
like the rest. The heathen allies at last were
thoroughly aroused. With the wildest enthusiasm
they snatched the proffered hatchet and swore war to
the death against the common enemy.

Then came a solemn war-feast. Barrels of wine
with abundant supplies of tobacco were served out
to the guests. Two oxen and several large dogs had
been chopped to pieces for the occasion and boiled
with a quantity of prunes. Kettles were carried in,
and their steaming contents ladled into the wooden
bowls with which each provident guest had supplied
himself. Seated in a ring on the grass, the Indians
began eagerly to devour the food placed before them.
It was a point of conscience not to flinch, and they
gorged themselves until they fairly choked with re-
pletion. It was not a pleasant sight, yet the colonists
regarded it with some complacency, seeing that it
meant prosperity and security against danger.

CHAPTER XI.

THE ANNUAL FAIR.

THE following day witnessed the opening of the great Annual Fair. Trade was in full activity; never had Canada known a more prosperous commerce than now in the midst of her dangers and tribulations. That very morning, to the overwhelming joy of the citizens of Ville Marie, Le Durantaye, late Commandant at Michillimackinac, arrived with fifty canoes, manned by French traders and filled with valuable furs.

Merchants of high and low degree had brought up their most tempting goods from Quebec, and every inhabitant of Montreal of any substance sought by every means in his power to gain a share of the profit. The booths were set along the palisades of the town, and each had an expert interpreter, to whom the trader usually promised a certain portion of his gains. The payment was in card money—common playing cards—each stamped with a crown and a *fleur de lys*. The newly arrived French bushrangers were the heroes of the hour and appeared to enjoy their popularity. All the taverns were full. The coureurs de bois conducted themselves like the crew of a

man-of-war paid off after a long voyage, and their
fellow-countrymen, in the prevailing good-humor of
the moment, willingly condoned their excesses.
Many of them were painted and feathered like
their wild Indian companions, whose ways they
imitated with perfect success. Some appeared bru-
tally savage, but often their bronzed countenances
expressed only dare-devil courage and reckless gaiety.

"These gentry will live like lords, and set no
bounds to their revelry as long as their beaver-skins
last ; then they will starve till they can go off to the
countries up above there to seek a fresh supply.
Swaggering, spending all their gains on dress and
feasting, they even try to imagine themselves nobles,
and despise the honest peasants, whose daughters
they will not marry, even though they are themselves
peasant-born," said one priest to another, as he eyed
with evident disapproval the noisy, reckless crew.

The windows on St. Paul Street were thrown open
and crowded with ladies ; the benches before every
door were thronged. One woman of the poorer sort
had a half-dressed baby in her arms ; another a
lettuce that she was washing ; a third held a little
bowl of soup, which she ate in the street, gesticulating with such frantic energy that her sabots rattled
on the stones. All dreaded to lose any part of the
show.

The gathering about the market-place represented
all classes and conditions. There were merchants
engaged in serious negotiations, grave priests of St.

Sulpice, suave, smiling Jesuits, plump, good-humored Recollets. Gentlemen critically examined the crowd as it passed, exchanging salutations with friends and acquaintances, commenting with the slyest of chuckles upon the appearance of the ladies. Habitants, in plain, coarse attire, and their brown buxom wives, more gaily attired, chattered volubly. Indians stalked about with stoical and haughty composure. Children, in close caps without borders, and long-waisted gowns and vests, an exact imitation of the dress of their elders, shouted and gambolled with all the exuberance of youth. Plumed soldiers swaggered jauntily about, arquebus on shoulder. Licensed beggars abounded, wearing ostentatiously their certificate of poverty signed by some local judge or curé. French musicians with drum, trumpet and cymbal did their best to swell the tumult.

"All this tintamarre presages well for the colony," decided Nanon as she followed her mistress. "Beaverskins and trade and money, it means absolutely the same thing, and all good in their way. I like not the way things are going, either. My poor little generous demoiselle! That soft, sleek, splendid cat of an English girl, for all her feigned innocence, still makes eyes at the Sieur du Chesne. Is it only I who have eyes to spy her tricks? For me, I waste not my breath on the melancholy; no patience have I for jeremiads. Tell not your secret in the eyes of the cat, but it is I, Nanon Benest, who will at once sew in the lappet of that gallant's coat an image of St.

Felix to secure him from charms and lead him in the right way. And it was I who dreaded the evil eye from the first."

"*Oui-da! oui-da!* we are in despair for time, my friends. Shall we then lose the chance of making a sou when it alights at our very door—we who have been breaking our hearts for trade so long," panted a stout woman, followed by two sturdy lads, as she resolutely pushed her way through the crowd. "Place, there, *ma bibiche*."

Nanon reddened and flouted like an enraged turkey gobbler at this unceremonious address.

"Thy *bibiche*! indeed, that were an honor to be coveted. I know thee, wife of Chauvin the younger, whose son Louis was turned back from his confirmation for running the woods when he should have been ringing the bells. And old Pepin, who is like a sour crab-apple. *Scaramouch!* knowest thou to whom thou speakest?"

The struggling, jesting, good-humored assembly found no lack of diversion. Two men, who had been arrested for theft, were exposed in the pillory, each having on his chest a record of the offence committed. One, a sturdy rogue to whom such correction was likely enough not a novelty, looked boldly around with a certain humorous appreciation of the situation; the other, younger and more sensitive to the shame of his position, sat with bowed head and downcast eyes, while a herald, after beating a drum to call attention to the announcement, proclaimed aloud : 113

8

"*De par le roi.* Know, then, nobles, citizens, peasants, that by order of His Majesty the King, Candide Bourdon and Xavier Cointet, accused and found guilty of theft, are condemned to two days in the pillory and two hundred livres damages, payable to the religious ladies of the Hotel-Dieu."

The crowd cast mud and abuse liberally at the culprits, and Migeon the bailiff, an imposing personage in the dignity of his uniform, contemplated the whole affair with an easy and affable air of proprietorship. Bayard the notary—a man of consequence in the town as being thoroughly conversant with everybody's business affairs; lean and brown and wrinkled, wearing narrow robes with a collar almost ecclesiastical in appearance, and waistband to match, whose brown wig in the ardor of controversy was constantly being pushed crooked—was settling a dispute between two traders, who in their eagerness seemed ready to tear the mediator to pieces. In another spot, to the intense delight of the populace, the effigies of two Indians were being consumed in a roaring fire. Sentence of death had been passed upon two savages, who, escaping, had regained their native haunts. Justice therefore for the moment was obliged to content herself with wreaking vengeance upon their inanimate representatives.

Amid all this throng du Chesne found friends and companions of every degree. His father, a man of sound rather than brilliant qualities, was respected, but was too cautious and distrustful to be liked

except by those who knew him well. His brother
Pierre was reverenced as a saint but despised as a
man. It was du Chesne who monopolized the popularity accorded to the family. His charming light-
ness of manner expressed confidence rather than
carelessness; he was interested in everybody's concerns and carried about with him a buoyancy of
spirit which acted like a tonic upon all with whom he
came in contact.

Jean Ameron, Le Ber's valet, was describing to a
soldier recently arrived from France the burning of
four Indians, which had taken place not long before
at the Jesuit Square.

"This is nothing to look at," pointing to the
squirming bundles of clothes rapidly being consumed
by the flames. "These people of whom I am telling
you exhibited a marvellous courage and endurance.
That is the Indian fashion. But, see you, faith of
Jean Ameron, that was something to laugh at.
Their agony lasted six hours, during which they
never ceased to sing their own warlike deeds. Four
brothers, they were, the largest and handsomest men
I ever saw."

"Burned to death?" inquired the soldier.

"No, not precisely that. It was a form of torment
the Indians themselves have invented. They were
tied to stakes, driven deep into the earth, and every
one of our savage allies, aye, and some Frenchmen,
too—in truth, I myself also took part in the affair,
and it requires courage to touch an Iroquois—even

when tied to a stake he might get loose, and their looks are like those of demons. Every one of us, believe you, armed himself with a piece of iron heated red-hot, with which we scorched all the bodies of the heathens from head to foot."

"Yes, fault of me, too-well treated were those pagans," interrupted a sunburnt voyageur, whose head was adorned with waving red feathers, "Drinking brandy that disappeared down their throats as quickly as though it had been poured into a hole made in the earth. They were provided with all they desired."

"Bah! that explains itself; the brandy was to deaden their sufferings," added a woman standing by. "Better chance had those heathens than many Christians. The Fathers baptized them, addressing merely a few brief words of exhortation (for to do more would be merely washing a death's head), and free from their sins they ascended straight to Heaven."

Suddenly, while trade and amusement were in the full tide of activity, high above the babble of chattering and bargaining and the echo of jovial laughter rose the death-cry. Instantly every sound and motion ceased; it was as though a sudden spell had fallen upon the busy gathering, an awed, breathless silence. Once, twice, eight times it was heard, rising and falling in weird cadences. Its significance was perfectly comprehended by the listeners, most of whom were habituated to modes of savage warfare. This was the signal given by a war-party returning in triumph with the scalps of eight enemies. Every man snatched his weapon, and for a time all was confusion. Among the authorities hurriedly whispered consultations took place, then, inspired by a sudden and irresistible impulse, soldiers, priests, traders, Indians, women and children, all rushed off in the direction whence the sound proceeded.

A man of gigantic stature, painted, greased and feathered like an Indian, and almost as swarthy of complexion, strode forward with a majestic air of composure, as though enjoying a happy sense of his own importance. In one hand he held eight long sticks from which were suspended a like number of lank waving tresses. In front of him, tied together like children in leading strings, walked two squaws with downcast eyes, whose resigned and stoical countenances looked as though carved out of wood.

"Who can this be?" each one asked his neighbor. "He is one of ours, a Frenchman."

Suddenly among the voyageurs a cry arose.

"It is Dubocq, or his spirit—no, it *is* Dubocq, yes, truly, Dubocq!" Then they raised a resounding shout of welcome—"Vive Dubocq! our brave Dubocq, our champion against our enemies!"

CHAPTER XII.

A CANADIAN BUSHRANGER.

DUBOCQ smiled condescendingly upon the enthusiasm with which his appearance was greeted; he accepted with sedateness the embraces and warm congratulations of his friends, but, perfectly conscious of his own dignity, resolutely refused to divulge any of the particulars of his story until he reached M. de Callière, Governor of Ville Marie.

Lydia, by nature timid, had no idea of controlling her fears when comfort and succor of an especially pleasant description were close at hand. She now clung to du Chesne for protection, her face irradiated by a lovely expression, half smiles, half tears. Did ever sculptor chisel a mouth where all sweet graces curved more bewitchingly? The young man noted the upward sweep of the long lashes, the exquisite flush deepening in the cheeks and melting into the warm whiteness of brow and chin and throat. How engaging this clinging helplessness was!

"He is a savage!" the English girl exclaimed with a shiver, "I shall never get over my terror of all Indians."

Du Chesne's glowing eyes rested on her face; the

fervent glance cheered and strengthened her. Lydia required to be supported constantly, and she enjoyed the exhilarating sensation.

"No, Mademoiselle, he is of our own country. His grandfather was a Frenchman from Normandy, who married a squaw, Marie Arontio, daughter of the first Huron chief baptized by the sainted Father de Breboeuf. Ah! Mademoiselle, but that was a martyr worthy of the faith! Sainte Marie Madeleine, a nun of the Ursulines, in Quebec, is Dubocq's sister. He has always been considered one of our best fighters, an adept in Indian modes of warfare, and a man of great courage and extraordinary strength. Some years ago he was taken prisoner by our enemies, and as time went on and nothing was heard of him, all believed him dead. That was a genuine loss for the colony; we could ill afford to spare one of our best champions; hence his return occasions so much rejoicing. He has contrived to escape the clutches of the most ferocious savages in the world, at whose hands he could expect nothing but agonizing torments."

The crowd, following the bushranger with shouts and cheers, proceeded up St. Joseph Street to the residence of M. de Callière. The Count de Frontenac, attended by several members of his suite, happened to be within. Disturbed by the noise, the party, led by M. de Callière, hurried to the door to inquire into the cause of the commotion.

"What have we here?" asked the Governor-

General, who possessed a singular faculty for endearing himself to the populace by being interested in all his surroundings.

"Dubocq! Dubocq has returned! Dubocq! Vive our champion, Dubocq!"

The forest rover with composed assurance advanced to exhibit his trophies, and in answer to the Governor's enquiries, recounted the history of his exploits with much natural eloquence.

"I was taken prisoner by the Iroquois," he began, "and for a long time I labored as their slave. They found my strength useful in many ways. For me, I devoured my heart in silence, M. le Comte, for no way of escape seemed possible, and if it was my fate to perish in the hands of those demons, why, there was no more to be said. So I was waiting with what patience I could muster for the fatal moment in which I was to be burnt alive. It happened on an occasion when I was engaged in hunting with eight braves and two squaws"—(here he indicated with a gesture his two female companions, who had never even raised their eyes or given the slightest indication that they knew their fate was trembling in the balance)—"we camped in a spot where they had hidden a quantity of liquor. Having been on two war expeditions in which they had performed prodigies of valor, they had succeeded in enriching themselves at their enemies' expense, and were at the time visiting the liquor as a rest and indulgence after much privation. Desiring to carry nothing with them but their arms and ammunition, they had been fasting for many days; so, as you may imagine, M. le Comte, those wolves were not inclined to be very abstemious."

"It is the custom of these pagans to swallow brandy at a gulp, easier than we take light wine at our most jovial parties," whispered Jean Ameron to his friend, who was a keenly interested spectator of all that was going on.

"After supper," continued the hero of the occasion, "they commenced drinking and singing, according to their own ideas of enjoyment. Considering me as a victim about to be sacrificed to their vengeance, they invited me to join their orgy, with the comforting assurance that it would be my last opportunity, as they had decided to put an end to me at once. Being for the moment all companions in pleasure, they sang loudly, with joyful hearts celebrating their victories. They persisted in forcing quantities of the liquor on me. Though in usual well inclined to drink, I restrained my inclination, knowing that should I become helpless my fate would be at once sealed. After raising the brandy to my mouth I allowed it to spill, and as the wigwam was illuminated only by the uncertain light of the fire, the savages did not notice my evasion of their hospitable intentions. By this means I retained my composure, while by the middle of the night my companions, whose heads were heated by drink and the war-songs they had sung, were overcome by sleep. I made no movement, but feigned to be the drunkest of all the party, though watching quietly like a fox. Faith of Dubocq! the Iroquois and I, we know each other well, and here it was a question of life and death. I debated seriously whether when I found them all helpless, completely at my mercy, I should profit at once by my liberty, or whether before leaving I should send those ten heathen to the land of souls. As for the braves, that meant eight enemies less for the colony. Then, M. le Gouverneur, ladies, gentlemen and friends," with a grandiloquent flourish of the hand towards the unhappy prisoners, who still stood mute, like bronzed images of resignation, " then I resolved to spare these women as being unworthy a man's vengeance, and also as witnesses of my triumph.

" *V'la !* I commenced by tying the squaws tightly together, comprehending well that, having smaller brains than the men, they were more easily intoxicated and consequently more difficult to awaken. And, I assure you, they had not stinted themselves in the use of the liquor. I resolved to make sure, however, trusting my fate to no chance which I had power to provide against. In order to try if their sleep were really so profound as it appeared, I held pieces of flaming wood close to their faces; but, behold! not a movement, not so much as the quiver of an eyelash. My opportunity had come ; it but depended upon the strength of my own arm to escape death by torture. I have seen that ; I know what it is ; so do many of you, my friends."

The crowd responded to this appeal by a quick sympathetic murmur.

"Many of us have witnessed the death of our comrades, many bear scars of the wounds inflicted by those wolves. That thought nerved my heart. Arming myself with a heavy hatchet, I dealt one warrior after another a deadly blow, and that with the greatest rapidity. If one should awaken and give the alarm, then I was lost. *Tiens!* it was all finished in a crack. It was a cold butchery, I grant you, M. le Comte, but what will you, then? The choice lay between my death and theirs. Imagine to yourself when a man fights in the name of his lord the King, his Lord God, the holy saints and angels, and his own safety. I owed the Iroquois many a debt, and I endeavored honestly to pay them all.

"I tried vainly to awaken the two women, who still slept soundly. Then I sat down to smoke my pipe and indulge in many pleasant memories of the home which I had never thought to see again. We had still a long and dangerous journey before us, so it was necessary to set about making preparations. Next morning when the two women regained their senses I allowed them to perceive that a change had taken place in the position of affairs—that they had at the one stroke become widows and my slaves. I could not suppose that they were pleased by the course of events, but they said little. I assured them that I would spare their lives on condition that they would bear witness to the truth of my story, and they agreed with the best possible resignation. I may make them my compliments on their docility; never have they troubled me with useless lamentations. When I had adjusted my scalps to my taste—and you will perceive, M. le Comte, that they are arranged in true savage fashion—I took them and my prisoners and started upon my journey."

"Vive, Dubocq, who has killed eight Iroquois at a blow! Vive Dubocq!" shouted the excited and sympathetic crowd.

"But they are monsters! One hears only of shedding of blood." In her agitation Lydia had seized hold of du Chesne's hand, at which a thrill went through the young man's veins.

"All this is far removed from you; it is not fit that you should hear such tales. You should be surrounded by scenes of peace and tenderness. Cannot you trust yourself to my care, my sweet Lydia?" he urged tenderly.

The young Canadian felt himself completely fascinated by this fair childish beauty. There was something in the girl's guileless expression, the sight of her hair flowing in waves of gold over the shapely shoulders, that ensnared his heart. Then his efforts at consolation were so very successful, and were so gratefully received, that he could not fail to be thoroughly satisfied. Diane de Monesthrol might accept tribute of general admiration if it pleased her to do so; for his part, he preferred the sweetly feminine creature who was pleased to receive rather than confer distinction.

Frontenac, himself a brave man, had always shown

cordial sympathy for the reckless courage of the voyageurs and bushrangers. He now readily gave utterance to his commendations.

"Ta, ta, ta! bravely done, my fine fellow. These are the sort of defenders that Canada requires; would that we had many more of them. Eight enemies killed at a stroke! He is a Canadian hero; we owe him the thanks of the colony."

"*Et par le corbeau,*" grumbled Jean Ameron, who made desperate but futile attempts to imitate the soldiers in the jaunty swagger of their manner. "Heroes, like saints, are cheap in this country. To kill eight Iroquois, that were easily enough done— just one sharp blow skilfully directed, and all is over. Little more effort is required than for killing a mouse. Thirty livres, no less, is the price paid for each scalp; two hundred and forty livres will this bird of prey receive from the Government. It was but chance that placed the occasion in Dubocq's way. Some are favored by luck; I could myself do as much as that."

"Jean, my friend, thou art not of those whose light is suffered to hide under bushels," protested the soldier.

"Maitre Bourdon, hast thou good wine at thy tavern?" demanded Frontenac.

"But yes, plenty, and of the most excellent, M. le Comte; of many kinds also, to suit all tastes—Vin de Grève, both the white and the red, wine of Xeres,

Muscat —" the little fat man was delighted to seize the opportunity of proclaiming the prime quality of his wares.

"Drink, then, my friends, to the health of His Majesty, and to that of the brave Dubocq, not forgetting the prosperity of Canada, and confusion to our enemies, the Iroquois!"

CHAPTER XIII.

PIERRE'S TEMPTATION.

THE grounds attached to Jacques Le Ber's house were laid out partly as a flower and partly as a kitchen garden. They were divided by broad gravelled walks, bordered with fragrant herbs and deliciously sweet old-fashioned plants. Orange and oleander trees in green boxes stood here and there. Along the side of the wall grew pear trees, currant bushes and grape vines. Sweetness of fragrance and brilliancy of color were everywhere.

Over the garden one morning had hung a dense fog, which, lifting, revealed radiant glimpses of blue sky, distant mountain and shining river. The trees, silvered by the light, seemed to rush gladly out of the mist, and the still fleeing remnants of vapor gave grace and movement to every object over which their trembling shadows passed. The air was sweet with growth and blossom, glad with song of birds, quiver of leaves, and flicker of sunshine and shadow. Pierre Le Ber, strolling leisurely down a shady path with his breviary in his hands, his lips moving in silent prayer, resolutely strove to steel his heart against all the harmonies of nature. His tall, slight figure,

emaciated by ceaseless vigils and penances, showed
the high and narrow forehead, thin-lipped sensitive
mouth, and deep dreamy eyes of the enthusiast.
As he walked the sound of a tender lullaby broke
upon his meditations. Instead of soothing him, however, the gentle strains seemed to produce a strangely
disturbing effect upon the ascetic's mind. His brow
showed deep corrugations, his lips were compressed
in quick irritation. With the warm sunshine and the
fresh morning air, laden with the scent of opening
blossoms, there seemed to glide into his senses, to
thrill through every vein and nerve, an instinct of
hope and consciousness of pleasure, a sensation of
peace and easy indulgence alluring as a child's dream.
He had been troubled in mind ; now the very air he
breathed seemed to offer consolation. Vainly he tried
to forget that he was still young, and that the world
was beautiful. He was impatient of his own thoughts,
and filled with indignant astonishment that after
ceaseless efforts to suppress the claims of the body
such trifles should have power to occupy his mind.

As these thoughts crowded upon poor Pierre he
made a violent effort to fling them from him as something intrusive. He would go away, he would resist
this entrancing influence. Turning hastily he found
himself close to Diane de Monesthrol. She was
carrying, easily and lightly, little Léon, the crippled
orphan whose parents had both perished at the massacre of Le Chesnaye, and who had himself been
grievously maimed by blows from an Indian toma-

hawk. His spine was injured, and he had but now been suffering from one of those paroxysms of pain which occasionally tortured him. The violence of the attack over, the child, soothed and exhausted, was falling asleep; the heavy blue-veined lids were slowly closing, while the girl bent over him with wistful tenderness. She laid the little one down beneath the shade of a wide-spreading tree, supported by cushions, and then, as she turned, encountered Pierre's earnest gaze. Le Ber's eldest son was seized with a sincere conviction that he would be better away from his father's beautiful ward, yet he stood silent, rooted to the spot.

Life just then to Diane was a vague, sweet chaos. Rejoicing in the strength of her ardent youth, it was not easy to accept existence calmly and tranquilly. Every day the sunshine seemed brighter, the sky above her more blue. It was always to her an amusement to tantalize and provoke Pierre, who was curiously sensitive to every girlish taunt. Professing as he did to despise feminine charms, it seemed a frolic to the girl to show him that he was not so invulnerable as he chose to fancy himself. Diane was aware that Anne Barroy was peering anxiously from a side window, and Anne's sharp, jealous eyes had already detected the weakness which the young man could never have been brought to acknowledge. It was like a child heedlessly playing with fire, for she had formed no conception of what strong human passion might mean. Just to tease Pierre was the

9

impulse of the moment—a thing which she had done a hundred times before and never bestowed a thought upon. Long years afterwards, looking back on her life, it seemed to Diane that on that fragrant summer day, in Le Ber's sunny garden, she had taken leave forever of her free and careless youth.

"It is thus I would always see you, Diane," Pierre exclaimed eagerly, "engaged in works of charity."

"I take charge of the little Léon simply because Nanon is occupied with Madame la Marquise," Mademoiselle de Monesthrol explained carelessly.

"You spend so much time and thought on those things which are unworthy of you," the young man could not forbear exhorting her, "lace and low dresses, fontanges and strange trinkets, the immodest curls expressly forbidden by St. Peter and St. Paul, as well as by all the Fathers and Doctors of the Church, the pomp of sin, the favorite devices of Satan. In their wish to please men, women make themselves the instruments and captives of the arch fiend."

Diane flashed a swift, bright, audacious glance at him.

"Do the ladies try to win your favor, cousin? I thought they all feared you. You must acknowledge I have never shown any desire to please you."

In the still sunny air, in the warmth and glow of a life which he could not stifle, standing face to face with the loveliest eyes he had ever seen, Pierre found himself engaged in an unusual conflict, and felt he must utter a vehement protest against the fatal, alluring attraction. The peculiar susceptibility to impressions which rendered him pliant to priestly influence also gave rise to endless complications against which he had no defence.

"Cast from you that levity destructive to the soul," he urged.

"But it is levity that I delight in," she replied, tapping a dainty high-heeled shoe upon the gravelled walk. "One can be young but once. When old age overtakes me I shall devote myself to good works. When that time comes then shall we, perhaps, be better friends; at that season I may perchance enjoy your sermons, cousin."

Pierre strove hard to maintain his tone of gentle superiority and to continue the discussion on a line of persuasive argument, but he was nervously impatient. A tinge of uncertainty was shadowed in his manner, a tumultuous excitement, a badgered, hopeless, still struggling shame. It was not often that he had the opportunity of holding a long conversation with the girl; he felt obliged to make the best of the occasion.

"That is the doctrine of the devil. Canada is indeed the fold of Christ, but the hosts of this world are beleaguering the sanctuary. Diane, is the glory of the Church to suffer prejudice from your actions? We are in the midst of sin. Remember that death is close at hand."

These words jarred upon Diane's mood. She resented Pierre's air of dissatisfied inspection, his assumption that his own judgment must be fundamentally and eternally right.

"Then let me be happy while I may. All have not the vocation to be saints and martyrs. We are young, the sun shines, life is fair and sweet, and God is good."

Pierre looked at her in evident anger, the wrathful disguise of tortured love. His reason was hampered in its action. He was unable to exercise any discriminating faculty. There was something pathetic in his insistence, for he plainly perceived that his importunities were unavailing. His desire for sympathy was so urgent and all occupying that he could not thrust it aside. The proud, untamable creature, so arch, so kind, so generous, with her whims and caprices and beauty, alive with spirit and energy, seemed to him the embodiment of all he had renounced. Had he only the power to mould her into an entirely different form, to convert her into a bloodless personification of sanctity, he was convinced that he would be saving her soul.

"Diane,"—he could not control the quivering of his voice—"Diane, the Holy Virgin will transform into angels all those who have the happiness to abandon the cares of this life. Will you not drink of the living and abounding waters of grace which have flowed so benignly over this land of New France? Misfortune is about to fall upon this household, how or when I have no power to tell, but it is sorrow and death; when I would pray, a dark presentiment weighs my spirit to the earth—there is no escape from it. Diane," he cried with yearning entreaty, "though you have cast in your lot with the world, the robe of God's saints awaits you; but that means suffering deep and terrible, the crucifixion of what is dearest. In my dreams you are ever present, but always among the holy ones, crowned with the exceeding glory of the martyrs worn only by those who have reached the fairest ideal of heaven's attainment, who have risen above all earthly joys and affections."

Diane was confused and awed, and withal much annoyed, at this address. It did not touch her as it might have done a woman of wider experience. She had a just faith in her own instincts, and was possessed of all the happy confidence of youth. What had she to do with suffering and misery? she, Diane de Monesthrol, surrounded by affection, to whom the plant of life was daily blossoming out into fuller perfection, the happiest girl in all the colony of New France.

"Oh! listen then, cousin, to the tumult in the street." Diane was delighted at the diversion. "Is it the voyageurs? nay, but it is the gentlemen."

> " *Vive Henri Quatre,*
> *Vive le Roi Vaillant,*
> *Ce diable à quatre*
> *A le triple talent*
> *De boire and de battre*
> *Et d'être un vert galant.*"

The jovial strains of the chorus broke on the stillness of the garden like a disturbing influence.

"And the music, cousin, how entrancingly gay! When I hear the music I must dance; the desire is stronger than I."

Inspired by an impulse of wild mirth and the love of frolic, enlivened by the knowledge that Anne Barroy still kept an inquisitive watch at her shaded window, Diane began to circle and pirouette around the astonished young man. Gradually she surrendered herself to the influence of the music, allowing its rhythm to govern her movements. The lithe young form fell into flexible attitudes; it was a delight to mark the exquisite grace of her gestures, the suppleness of her limbs, the action of her swiftly twinkling feet. This was no wild whirl of abandonment; the smooth, swaying movement was stately and dignified; but to Pierre it meant the essence of sorcery. Was ever fairer creature formed? Her attractions were vivid, imperious, irresistible.

Diane herself was full of intense sensation and susceptibility to every new impression. The color deepened in her soft cheeks. She was no longer a heedless, guileless child; the soul of a woman, ardent and seductive, flamed in her sweet blue eyes. Pierre flushed with sudden mortification. For an instant he hated the girl and hated himself. His glance, first gently pleading, then sternly disapproving, changed swiftly to some keener emotion. He had been tolerably calm until he reached this point, then the blood began to course hotly through his veins; he found himself drifting upon wild unknown currents, carried beyond the safe limits of ecclesiastical restraint.

"Diane! Diane!" he cried, breaking in suddenly as if suffocated. All the girlish fun and mischief faded out of her eyes, Diane de Monesthrol's cheeks flamed with shame and fierce resentment. What did this new light of revelation mean? In her carelessness had she cruelly injured the son of one who had been her protector? Who was Pierre that he should dare to look at her with such eyes? She could have killed him as he stood. With the keen quivering of heart and soul she gained a glimpse of some of the deeper things of life.

"*Hola!* Diane and—and Pierre!" As he parted the branches of the thicket and stood revealed before the actors in this extraordinary scene, his surprise quite as great as their own, du Chesne's expression of utter consternation was so extremely comic that Diane broke into peals of ringing laughter.

This added the last touch to Pierre's misery. A sudden panic and horror seized him, furrowing his countenance as if with the action of years. As his brother's frank glance rested on him, giddy, as if buffeted by wind and tide in the midst of heat and passion, he paused with a convulsive shiver. He was conscious of falling from a great height to dread discomfiture and humiliation. The girl's beauty had kindled an emotion which glowed in his brain, leaped like wildfire from conjecture to conclusion, and carried all before it in an irresistible exhilaration. This was succeeded by the inevitable reaction. A sob, suppressed yet unrestrainable, escaped him. All three, the girl and the two young men, moved by a common instinct, glanced apprehensively up at the window where, from the heights of superior sanctity, the recluse might be looking down upon the trivial worldly passions and interests of her kindred. Pierre disappeared. Diane would have been glad to do the same, but mentally pulling herself together she conquered the cowardly impulse and sank panting down on the grass, shamed to the depths of her soul by du Chesne's look of mingled wonder and reproach.

CHAPTER XIV.

AN AWAKENING.

"WAS it a new step you were teaching him?" asked du Chesne. "But, no, it cannot be —not Pierre, who disapproves of worldly amusements."

"That melancholy death's head of a Pierre, he professes to despise women ; he is never content with me ; he has dared to sermonize me and I punished him," Diane roused herself to explain defiantly, instinctively resenting the youth's questioning gaze.

"But, Pierre—I cannot understand—Pierre is a saint—he will scarcely raise his eyes to look at any human being—his lips utter only prayers."

"And they are indeed detestable, these saints," she returned petulantly.

"Surely you would respect the virtues of those holy ones. We may not be very perfect, we others, but they accumulate perfections for us. Who can say how much we owe them?"

Du Chesne was staunch to his teaching and traditions. His voice had a caressing sound when he spoke to women. A smile now parted his lips as he threw himself on the grass beside her.

"Pierre is like other men," Diane exclaimed with laconic positiveness.

The audacity of the reply startled the young man. He watched her with eager, wistful scrutiny. Du Chesne was not an intellectual man, but his perceptions were swift and keen. Could it be possible that Diane loved Pierre, and that this affection had rendered her insensible to the attractions of the numerous lovers who had already sighed at her feet? It was a startling supposition, overturning some of his fixed ideas, but it would certainly account for many of the caprices which had puzzled him. He was loyal to the core, with a jealous and fervid allegiance both to his brother and to the girl who had held the place of a sister. Pierre was bound by solemn vows to an ascetic life—could he be willing to decline to what he would choose to consider a lower plane? Diane's affection was certainly a prize worth obtaining. No doubt it would all come right in some way. The glamor proceeding from the indefinite brightness of youth, certain bewitching and yet intangible possibilities which had enthralled his own imagination, disposed him to accept the most hopeful view of the situation. And, after all, the hypothesis might not be built on sufficient foundation.

"And Crisasi, too," he continued, speaking without reflection, awkwardly and anxiously. There were curious lines of perplexity on his brow.

"Oh! the Chevalier is really too absurd; at his best he is only doleful—never amusing. And you know it is the plain duty of a man to show himself amusing." Diane strove to speak lightly, notwithstanding the rising tremor in her throat. Why should there be any restraint in the frank, pleasant comradeship which had united them since childhood? Du Chesne plainly comprehended none. He was so kind, so cordial, so honestly satisfied with his own good intentions, that it was difficult to hold him at a distance. He held an inveterate objection to inconsistencies of every description, and tried to reconcile two apparently conflicting tendencies in the girl, to whom he was sincerely attached. A vague resolve that had been floating through his mind suddenly assumed definite proportions.

"Crisasi is a brave and gallant gentleman; none in the colony is more respected. If amusement is a necessity, choose such fops as d'Ordieux, and leave alone the men you have power to pain. Spare the Chevalier, Diane, he is a disappointed and heartbroken man."

"You are as bad as Pierre! That is not like you, du Chesne." Mademoiselle de Monesthrol was suddenly aroused. The blood in a rich carmine flood mantled over her delicate face; her eyes dilated, deepened, darkened, until their soft blue changed to black. What was this man's frankly expressed disapproval to her that she should thrill and tremble at his words. A terrible dread, latent in her heart, now ran through her throbbing veins, her entire being quickened by that thrill of feeling which is at once sweetness and keenest pain. A sentiment which she disowned, which she had fought desperately and persistently, inch by inch, had conquered; yet to hide the wound, to hold up her head, smiling, and, if need be, die hiding it, was the first natural instinct. She did not speak, for her heart was fluttering to her lips and she could not utter a word. Yet to the tender-hearted, wilful creature there was an excitement in the consciousness of peril. Detection might be worse than death; still to dare discovery, to push danger to the very verge of exposure, furnished a thrilling agitation which offered relief from pain. Raising her head, as though courting rather than avoiding scrutiny, she met du Chesne's searching gaze with cool nonchalance.

"*Sainte Dame!* and what is that to me?" with a gesture of haughty repudiation. "Were I answerable for the disappointments of every gentleman of New France my lot would be indeed a sad one."

The clear tones of gentle disdain irritated the young Canadian. He could scarcely restrain a movement of impetuous anger; and yet, with the characteristic trust of his nature, he tried to believe the best.

"Diane, you know not of what you speak. It is your inexperience that causes you to appear cruel. Why, I remember you cried yourself sick when your bird died, and again when Bibelot's paw was hurt— and then the devotion with which you have attended little Léon shows you are no heartless woman. It may be your time has not yet come When it comes, as it surely will, you will then comprehend the meaning of true love—the happiness, the suffering, the trust and faith." He spoke eagerly, his glowing boyish heart shining in his eyes. Diane could not mistake the evidence of that fire out of which love is born; her doubt and pride were suddenly swept away. She had no power to confront this precious and bewildering possibility. All existence was suddenly raised to brilliancy and interest, as with a sparkling draught of sunlit elixir.

In a little closet off from Mademoiselle de Monesthrol's chamber stood a miniature altar. A fair ivory image of Our Lady of Sorrows gleamed white amidst the environment of gorgeous color; a richly chased silver lamp burned dimly before it, and a jar of spotless lilies was set beside the *prie-dieu* with its velvet hassock and Book of Hours. In a fervor of devotion the girl sank down before the altar.

"Holy Virgin, bless me! Make me worthy of the great happiness thou hast given me."

CHAPTER XV.

NANON'S LOVERS.

MARRIAGEABLE women were at a premium in the colony. Nanon in her comeliness, activity, and audacity had since her arrival in New France attracted many lovers. Most of these followed her for a while, then, discouraged by her disdain, fell away from their allegiance and married some meeker damsel. The two who had remained most persistently faithful to her charms, patiently enduring her tempers and caprices year after year, were Jean the valet and Baptiste Leroux, familiarly known as Bras de Fer.

Baptiste was an enormous man, over six feet two in height, and stout in proportion. His round face expressed an exaggeration of simplicity. His beard was black, but the long hair he wore floating on his shoulders was a warm auburn. His eyes, which were nearly always half closed, gave him the appearance of stupidity; but when moved by any unusual emotion they opened wide, their keen brightness changing the whole character of his countenance. The extreme slowness of his movements imparted an air of apathetic indolence to the massive frame. He wore a striped blue shirt and grey trousers, with a red sash

knotted around his waist, its fringed ends hanging
down on the left side. On his head, winter and
summer, was a beaver cap. His feet were protected
by Indian boots, the upper part, of sheepskin, drawn
up over the trousers, and fastened under the knee by
narrow strips of sealskin. The sleeves of his jacket
were turned up at the elbows, displaying a pair of
huge muscular arms tattooed curiously. Malicious
people sometimes insinuated that all the good fellow's
force lay in his physical powers, and that his intellectual faculties were not of the brightest.

The eldest of a family of nineteen children born to
a poor colonist, Baptiste had been obliged from early
childhood to make his way through the world as best
he could. When still a very young lad he had
entered Le Ber's service, where later he had shared
the games and escapades of du Chesne and his
cousins, the young le Moynes, teaching the boys the
secrets of woodcraft and the delights of forest life.
Afterwards he became a noted coureur de bois,
wandering at will through the trackless woods of
Canada, the great North-West and Louisiana, camp-
ing, hunting, fishing, fighting, everywhere renowned
among white men and Indians for his unerring skill
as a marksman and his extraordinary strength and
courage. When severe laws were enacted against the
bushrangers, prohibiting that lawless, delightful freedom of the wilderness to which his heart ever clung,
Leroux again took service with the Le Ber family, for
whom he felt an unswerving devotion. Among the

colonists many marvellous tales concerning Bras de Fer's adventures were told. Even allowing for the exaggeration of national pride, it must be admitted that many of these stories had a substantial foundation in fact.

Once it happened that on the shores of Lake Champlain Baptiste and a younger brother were taken prisoners by the Iroquois. The Indians, in triumph at having secured so redoubtable an adversary, fastened their captives to two oaken stakes planted firmly in the ground. Fancying that Bras de Fer, who was much the stronger of the two, would endure torture the longer, they selected the brother as their first victim. A savage heated his hatchet red hot and applied it to the boy's naked breast. Baptiste, resigned to his fate, had prepared to chant his death-song with a stoicism borrowed from his Iroquois foes, but the sight of his brother's torture roused him to superhuman effort.

"Forty thousand tribes of demons!" he shouted, bending himself double, and by a supreme effort bursting the bonds that held him ; then tearing the stake out of the earth, with it he struck down four of the Iroquois in quick succession. The assault was so unexpected, and his attitude so terrifying, that the remainder of the party, believing in their consternation that they were attacked by a species of avenging Manitou, swiftly fled, leaving Baptiste and his brother to make their way home undisturbed.

All Bras de Fer's brave exploits, his renown, or the

friendly consideration with which his employers treated him, seemed unavailing to give him advantage over his voluble rival. Baptiste was far too modest to boast of his own merits, and Jean was only too ready to vaunt imaginary virtues which he liberally attributed to himself. Nanon accepted the homage of both in a sharp, imperious, scornful way, never directly favoring either. Through all Baptiste endured the most hopeless jealousy of Jean's fluent, deceiving tongue.

"Aye," Jean declared easily and lightly, "It is the taste of Nanon, as of all women, to coquette. It is their privilege, and I for one would not deny it to them."

His charmer was never without a ready retort.

"Aye, as it is the wont of all men to be fools and heartless apes, to run to death after any proud turkey, and never to perceive those of real worth."

Nothing daunted, Jean continued to smoke his pipe reflectively.

"I have never been greatly inclined to matrimony myself. When I picture the perils through which I have passed—aye, I myself, Jean Ameron—with damsels of every description to choose from, brown and blonde, fat and lean, tall and short, all awaiting but a look, and some not absolutely ill-favored ; one, indeed, with a barrel of bacon entirely her own, was offered me, but I found myself obliged to decline, my friends trying in vain to persuade me to accept the King's gift."

Bras de Fer was taking his supper in the same room. In general the stalwart voyageur had an inordinate capacity for devouring the various colonial dainties, such as eels in sailor guise, pigeons with cabbages, partridges served with onions, soup with plums, eggs and tripe, brown bread and cheese. He had been hungry when he entered the house, but the Frenchman's facility of utterance quite reduced the big Canadian's enjoyment of his food. Were he but master of such captivating eloquence he might long ago have won the desire of his heart. Nanon never appeared more attractive. Her full lips took a richer red, a livelier crimson suffused her sunburnt cheek, there was a dancing merriment in her bright, dark eyes as she asked demurely :

"Was it not the damsels who escaped so sad a fate? To me it is equal. I see on every side husbands and wives who quarrel and spit at each other like cats, and where is the gain, my heart? In this country it is not difficult to marry. Brown and lean as a weasel is Mam'selle Anne, yet even she could become a wife if she would."

Baptiste felt that to sit silently listening was the hardest trial he had ever endured. He had been no stranger to manifold dangers and adventures, having served as guide in nine expeditions against the Five Cantons. He had killed with his own hand more than sixty Iroquois, had twice been tied to the stake waiting to be burned alive ; had bravely sung the death-song, while the joints of two of his fingers had

been broken, after they had been smoked in an Indian
pipe ; had in genuine savage fashion learned to mock
at his own torments, when a necklace of hatchets,
heated red hot, had been suspended round his neck,
causing wounds of which he still kept the scars ; yet
with all this his valor failed him when he had most
need of it. He could have demolished his paltry
rival at a blow, yet he dared not contemplate the
possibility of having Nanon turn on him with scorn
and anger.

"Nanon!"

By a tremendous effort Baptiste concentrated his
will. Rising, he left his untasted supper with the determination to crush his rival's pretensions, plead his
own suit, or perish in the attempt! At the impassioned utterance of her name the girl quickly turned
her head. When he felt the sharp, bright glance of
his beloved resting upon him, the giant's courage
oozed away. With a long drawn sigh he sank back
on his chair disconsolately.

"If you please, Bras de Fer?" Nanon inquired
politely.

Baptiste shook his head with the most helpless and
mournful resignation ; both ideas and words had
escaped him ; he felt himself turning hot and cold
all over as he gazed at her deprecatingly. Nanon
shrugged her plump shoulders with an air of amused
amazement.

"What wouldst thou say, Bras de Fer? Surely
thou wouldst not make sugar-plum compliments like

those of Jean? Is it the week of the three Thursdays, that thou shouldst attempt to make compliments? Even Balaam's ass had the power of speech conferred upon it at times, but thine eloquence is overpowering. Ta, ta, ta! there would be no peace in Paradise if thou wert there, unless thou couldst contrive to mend thy manners, my friend." Nanon's brown face dimpled with coquettish smiles, and Jean indulged in a malicious grin for which the Canadian could have found it in his heart to slay him.

"It was constancy to thy attractions, it was disinclination to marriage with another, that prevented me from entering the forest, engaging in warfare against the Iroquois, becoming a renowned fighter, and making my fortune in the fur trade," pursued the imperturbable Jean.

"Think, then, and is it truly so?" Nanon interposed with exasperating simplicity, "and I had really believed that it was thine own cowardice that made thee prefer the ease of home to ranging the woods with the savages and wild beasts."

"Indeed, yes, such is really the case. A cow, a pair of swine, a pair of fowls, two barrels of salted meat, and eleven crowns in good money have my own constancy and thine hard-heartedness cost me. Surely some recompense may be considered my due. And during all these long years I have been pursued by a frightful nightmare, a dream of awakening to find myself a husband against my will. Consider how sad a fate, my good Nanon; and when once the ceremony is performed, no redress, for when the Church binds she ties fast ; one fastens a knot with the tongue which the hands cannot untie."

Nanon smiled complacently upon all this, until Baptiste, who felt that he had reached the extreme limit of endurance, rushed out. Then the girl promptly gathered up her work and prepared to ascend to her mistress's apartment. Jean made another attempt to detain her.

"And Nanon, I have observation, me. I see many things. I would tell a secret but between ourselves. It is the blonde English demoiselle whom the Sieur du Chesne adores, and not the most noble the demoiselle de Monesthrol."

The ruddy peasant face flamed into fiery wrath. That her lady's attractions should be cheapened, that her pretensions should be slighted, infuriated the devoted maid. Such a dread had awakened in her own mind—would another dare to put it into words?

"Guard thy mouth! And is it a good-for-nothing of thy species who will dare to compare my demoiselle—the daughter of great nobles who fought and bled for the King—to any dirt of bourgeois? It is with such as the Comte de Frontenac—except that M. le Gouverneur has already had the ill-luck to make choice of a lady, and if report speaks true, of one not so admirable either—that our demoiselle should mate. *Bête* ! cease, then, thy bellowing and mend thy manners. Like a serpent thou wouldst bite the hand that nourishes thee."

In terror Jean fled from the storm he had evoked. Nanon stood wringing her hands and stamping her feet.

"In truth, I know not whether to weep like a watering-pot or to scratch somebody's eyes out. Ah! if I could but reach that craven-hearted wolf with my nails. The worst sting of all is that it is all true. And this English girl will pay him with his own coin, loving herself always best and last, with but small thought to spare for anyone else. My noble, proud mistress who smiles and is happy, seeing nothing, decking that other one in her best, and never weary of praising that one's beauty and sweetness. Sweetness?—it is the look of the cat at the cream. The neuvena I made in honor of that worthless St. Joseph, with the intention of securing our little lady's happiness, all goes for nothing. That useless image shall no longer delude innocent believers."

Like a whirlwind the serving-woman swept to the altar where stood the figure of St. Joseph, serenely unconscious of the enormity of his own offences, or of the storm which was about to descend upon him. It was the work of an instant to snatch him from his eminence, to shake and belabor him viciously, pouring out the while a flood of abuse as eloquently vituperative as a fertile brain and fluent tongue could devise, to rush down the garden and with all the strength inspired by fury to hurl him over the stone wall. Then, and then only, when her vengeance was accomplished, did Nanon pause for breath, drawing a long sigh of relief.

"Now shall my eyes, even mine, have the consolation of seeing that valueless saint lying in the dust shattered into a thousand pieces."

With a bang which was intended as a further vent for her distressed feelings, Nanon threw wide open the side gate leading from the secluded greenery of the garden into the dusty street. Then she stopped suddenly as though she had received a shock; the gleam of triumphant satisfaction faded from her eyes, her ruddy color turned to gray pallor. The ecclesiastical authorities would likely view with strong disfavor any disrespect paid to the saints; some thought of the consequences of her action began to penetrate Nanon's agitated mind.

Looking thoughtfully down at the fragments of the ill-used St. Joseph stood a priest. He was a large, powerfully-built man, in a narrow collar, long dusty black coat and three-cornered hat. As she met his kindly piercing gaze Nanon's wrath faded, and she bent her head while he raised his hands with a slight gesture of benediction before he blessed her. Her quick feminine intuition taught her that she would fare much better with this man than if she had fallen into the hands of the Jesuits. There were few in Ville Marie but had unqualified faith in the gigantic soldier priest, Father Dollier de Casson, Superior of the Seminary of St. Sulpice.

"Why, what is this? Didst thou imagine, my good Nanon, that the passers-by were heathen Iroquois, that thou shouldst assault them by means of the holy saints?"

Nanon in the excitement of the moment forgot her
fear and recovered her natural audacity. As she remembered her grievances her breast shook with great
sobs; for a second the passion struggling in her
throat could find no utterance. At last she broke
forth:

"The worthless, deceiving saint! My little noble,
gentle mistress, pure and guileless as the holy saints
themselves, cast aside for any tag of rubbish! Of all
the great and noble ladies whom God has sent into
this world to beautify His creation, to glorify His
name, and for the relief and happiness of their fellow-
creatures, none ever fulfilled the object of the Creator
more perfectly than our demoiselle. Yet, behold that
kite of an Anne, stuck all over with feathers of spite
and hypocrisy, her very look enough to turn milk
sour, and she boasts that she receives of the saints
every favor she demands. And if the saints fail us
what is to become of us poor common people who
have no other protection?"

The priest listened with silent attention to the confused, vehement recital. He was too thoroughly
versed in the intricacies of human nature not to
readily comprehend the faithful serving-woman's
meaning. He had himself a passion for duty and
discipline, a genius for command and obedience,
while his whole soul loathed dastards and renegades.
A good Christian, laboring manfully at his calling,
he had made the joys and sorrows, hopes and fears
of his flock his own. In the most cordial fashion he

worked for the people, dogmatized, and stormed at them, but, however strict to his ideal of duty, he never lost patience with human frailty.

"Ah, the good-for-nothing saint! Figure to yourself, my Father, a neuvena in his honor—never a word omitted though the poor bones ached and the eyes were drowsy with sleep—four candles burning perpetually before his altar, and all of the very best. Nothing did I grudge if only the little demoiselle could have her heart's desire. It was I that took her from the arms of her dying mother—me, but a slip of a girl myself—and she has been my charge, my first thought, ever since." Here beating her hands together, Nanon yielded to a new transport of exasperation.

The Sulpician cast a keen glance from under the white eyebrows which contrasted with his hale, sunburned face.

" *Voyons*, my daughter. You would desire high place and favor in this world for Mademoiselle de Monesthrol."

"Oh! but yes, my Father," she replied, coloring deeply, smoothing down her apron the while with her shapely brown hands. " Perhaps I have not the air of it, but I have seen things in my time. The people here know nothing of all that, but I remember the life over there in France. It is at the Court of our lord the King that my demoiselle should shine, among the great dames and brilliant demoiselles. Ah! that is what I would have for our little one.

To see all the world admire her state, but with reverence, be it understood ; to walk behind, to see and to share her glory, to repay the rebuffs we have received in our fallen fortunes, to hear it whispered as I pass, ' There goes Nanon, serving-woman to Her Grace, Madame la Duchesse de '—that is as it should be."

A smile of irrepressible humor curved de Casson's firm lips.

" Thou covetest this world's glory, yet thou wouldst grudge her high place in the Heavenly Kingdom. My brave and loyal Nanon, thou wouldst generously sacrifice much to win happiness for thy mistress. I also would it were God's will that the demoiselle should travel His way by a smooth and sunny road, but if there is no easier path to heaven, then bless her in taking that which is offered, my daughter. The roads leading to perfection are often dark and thorny."

" And that is what I cannot bear," sobbed Nanon, as the priest continued thoughtfully as though thinking aloud :

" To love is to serve. If service and affection are considered separately, the very essence of love, that which gives it life, is lost. After all, love, when unselfish, whether joyous or unfortunate in its results, must be splendid and lofty." Then recalling his attention by an effort he added, " Thy loyal affection, my good Nanon, is not as wise and tender as that of thy Master, who knows all things and judges

with clearer eyes than we poor mortals. Thine would
deprive Mademoiselle of the crown and grace of
suffering ; His will uphold her amidst the fiery ordeal
of tribulation. See to it, Nanon. Yield the child's
future up to the care of Him who is the loving
Father of all."

The clear tones had a sort of inspiring ring in
them ; the composed, benevolent countenance was
illumined by the cheering light of faith and courage.
Nanon hung her head. This philosophy, so high and
pure, was beyond her comprehension ; what she really
craved was assurance of success.

" What you say is doubtless all true, M. le Superior,
and it has the sound of beautiful language ; it is
suited to the quality, of that I am firmly convinced ;
but, faith of Nanon Benest, the heavenly glory is too
fine, too far off for such as I. I would rather that
other, me, that I could touch with the hands, and
talk about, and let all the world see. Let Mam'selle
Anne, who is ugly as a spider and cross as an enraged
sheep, keep the first ; I grudge it not. If M. le
Superior will but give himself the trouble to consider, he will certainly perceive that no one thinks of
the little one's interests but her own poor servant
Nanon. Madam la Marquise made the sacrifice of
all when she left her own country, and it appears
quite natural to her that others should do the same.
The Sieur Le Ber adores Mademoiselle, but keeps
steadily in mind his plans for ennobling his own
family. M. Pierre would have her a saint and a

martyr against her will, and now this English cuckoo has settled herself comfortably in Mademoiselle's own nest in order to pick the feathers from her at her ease."

" Thou wouldst undertake to play the part of Providence, and without having the means of doing so at thy disposal. *Va*, faithless one, it is well the good God should take the child's destiny out of thy rash and reckless hands. What signifies the mode to him who goes to glory—the shorter cut from the battlefield or a little longer way through a world of trouble? Thy loyal affection will be to thee a crown, but thy pride will prove a thorn to prick thee to the heart, my poor girl."

" Not that the most noble the demoiselle de Monesthrol could condescend to wed with the son of the bourgeois Le Ber"—Nanon hastened to qualify her rash admissions, and to vindicate her feminine right of having the last word ; " but of right he should kneel humbly at her feet, thankful for a glance or a gracious word."

CHAPTER XVI.

A VICE-REGAL BANQUET.

THE Count de Frontenac entertained the digni-
taries of the colony at one of those late suppers
which had been so severely denounced by the clerical
authorities, but which were so highly enjoyed by the
more worldly portion of the community. The service
of the table was arranged with elaborate magnificence.
Clusters of lights flashed on gold and silver plate.
The banquet consisted of four courses. Chicken soup
was served first ; then followed prime legs of mutton
garnished with chops, and choice venison pies whose
pale gold-colored crust was raised in fanciful shapes.
Between the roasts were dishes of plover, woodcock
and partridges roasted on the spit, and strings of
larks served by the half-dozen on the little splinters
of wood upon which they had been cooked. The
third course consisted of entrées, salads, both sweet
and salt, perfumed omelettes, blanc-manges, burnt
creams, fritters and fruit pies. The fourth was des-
sert, for which there were fruits piled in pyramids,
cakes, macaroons, march-paine and preserves of various kinds, the whole accompanied by the fashionable
French wines of the day.

As a host, stately, brilliant, imposing, the Governor-General was at his best. The winning grace that tempered his strenuous will, the delicate condescension of his bearing, charmed his guests, as they had ever the power to bind his own party into devoted adherence.

"A last toast before we leave the table: 'To the glory of our arms.' Help yourselves, gentlemen, and here's to you," carrying to his lips a golden goblet engraved with the family arms, "To the glory of our arms."

The guests bowed ceremoniously in acknowledgment, raising their goblets and repeating, "To the glory of our arms."

The room to which the company adjourned was a long drawing-room with curtains of the finest Turkey red, embossed with a damask pattern. The high carved mantel-piece was painted white. There were rich fauteuils and couches, buhl cabinets and spindle-legged chairs. On rosewood cabinets, inlaid with ivory, stood dainty Japanese jars filled with spices and dried rose-leaves.

The company was as brilliant as beauty and wit could render it. The fascination and marked individuality which have made of Frenchwomen a power, and rendered them an inspiration to the men of their race, stamped on all around them the impress of their aptitudes, their graces, their charm. Card-tables were set out; the older guests played at lasquenet, hombre, piquet and brélan; the younger members of the party

revelled in charades and *bouts-rimés*, or listened to the
soft strains of the théobe. In this charmed circle
Madame la Marquise reigned like an empress. Diane,
thoroughly in touch with her surroundings, had never
looked more beautiful. From the white and silver
brocade of her robe rose a regal head and neck;
beneath the powdered masses of hair her eyes burned
deeply like violet stars.

"The fairest favorite of Versailles cannot compare
with this peerless flower of New France!" declared the
Governor-General, who was considered a connoisseur
in feminine charms. "She has that in her face that
would send men to death as to a banquet."

"Mademoiselle, will you permit an old man whom
your freshness has made young again to pay his
devoirs? Your father was among my early friends,
as Madame la Marquise will bear me witness."
Frontenac made a low bow, his palms steadying his
sword, while his spurs clanked and his plumed hat,
held in the right hand, swept the ground. He spoke
the accepted language of gallantry, uttering the
strained courtesies of the Court and high society; but
the homage offered was palpably sincere, and carried
with it a subtle flattery.

The Chevalier de Crisasi held his place at
Mademoiselle de Monesthrol's side. The Chevalier
was owned body and soul by this girl; there was a
pathetic dignity in his very hopelessness. Even to
hint at his affection, under the present unfortunate
circumstances, would have been so glaring a departure

from French precedent that the courtly gentleman would have shrunk from attempting it. He could, however, express many varying meanings with his eyes, while the rest of his face remained blandly inexpressive ; the most rigid propriety could not deny him that privilege. The slow veiling of his eyes was like a silent salutation. Regarding the Chevalier with attention, Diane, by the aid of that new intuition which vitalized all her faculties, perceived a change in the man with whom in high spirits of girlhood she had carelessly trifled. Is this the misery of sleepless nights and weary days—the sick craving of a heart at variance with itself? A swift thrill of misgiving crossed her mind. Was it possible that her witcheries had helped to crush one upon whom the hand of misfortune had already been laid heavily?

"But she is a Circe, the Demoiselle de Monesthrol, a superb, magnificent creature whose spells are irresistible ; but, alas! without heart, without soul, like the coquettes of the Court," complained d'Ordieux, who found himself secluded from the circle which surrounded Diane, and whose views of matters in general were in consequence somewhat embittered.

"Ah! softly, my friend, softly, but what a comparison! Women of the Circe type to me offer no attraction. I prefer something simple and natural." Du Chesne laughed with easy frankness as his eyes turned to the spot where Lydia sat looking like a pale blush rose, childishly engrossed with all about her.

"'Simple and natural,' indeed. How you talk, my cousin. And who could be more simple and natural than our Diane? You are blind because you won't see," sharply interrupted Le Ber's niece, Madame de St. Rochs.

Wife and mother at thirteen, the little lady wore her matronly dignity with exaggerated demureness, or sometimes in the wild exhilaration of youthful spirits forgot it altogether. Now, with her piquant, mutinous face, she looked in her rich costume like some pretty, mischievous child masquerading in the stately robes of a grown woman.

"*Sainte Dame!* who so sweet to the old and the sick as Diane? who so patient with the little ones? When my baby—"

"When that baby's mother," mischievously interrupted du Chesne, his eyes twinkling with fun, "heartlessly abandoned the poor infant in order to enjoy the amusement of sliding with the children, Diane, moved to pity by its desolate condition, doubtless took the marmot under her protection. Say, then, is it not so, cousin?"

"Not at all, du Chesne. Could you believe so wicked a falsehood? I went only to see that no harm befell the little ones, and—"

"And were tempted to join in the amusements. What a situation for a matron of experience!" The young Canadian delighted in provoking his quick-tempered cousin. "And the doll, Cecile, that remained so long hidden in the old oak chest that

Armand, believing it a secret concealed from him, became wildly jealous. When the baby was ill, St. Rochs cradled the marmot on one knee and his wife on the other, singing soothing lullabies to the two babies at once. Was it not so, Cecile?" persisted her good-natured tormentor.

Madame de St. Rochs flushed angrily. Tears of vexation sprang to her eyes, though she made a determined effort to control herself.

"Say, then, Cecile, have you heard of the Indian witch who is camped at the foot of the mountain?" It was Diane de Monesthrol who came to the little mother's relief. "Strange things are told of her. She is said to have attained a marvellous age, and to be possessed of extraordinary powers."

"She foretold the disasters of the Sieur la Salle," said Crisasi.

"Let us organize a promenade to visit her," urged Madame de St. Rochs, who was immediately interested. "Baptiste Leroux can tell us all about her, and guide us to where she is to be found. He is as familiar with the Indian customs as with the five fingers of his hand. A genuine witch, and the sorcery practised by the natives is said to be of the worst possible kind. *Ciel!* let us go."

"Oh, fie! then, Cecile; such vagaries are unfitting a dignified matron. Your destiny is already settled. What would you more? A second husband before you are twenty?" The glimmer of laughter was shining in du Chesne's eyes, though his face was grave.

"Rest tranquil, cousin, it is about your fate I would concern myself. And, oh! there are a thousand things I would know. If Armand is soon to rise in the army?—we have indeed need of a larger income —and Diane? and the Chevalier? and the Sieur d'Ordieux?—yes, I would know what their fortunes are to be—and whether those wolves of Iroquois will end by devouring us all? I would know all." Madame de St. Rochs would not include Lydia, whose beauty and tractability had never won her favor, and against whom she had conceived a blind and inveterate prejudice.

"Are you so determined to obtain a glance into futurity, Cecile?" Diane's eyes sparkled with a glance of audacious fun. "Lydia will become a nun of the Congregation of Notre Dame. Cecile will be a great-grandmother before she is forty. The Chevalier will receive a command and win honor and renown. The Sieur d'Ordieux will regain his rights and appear as a great noble at the Court Armand will be a General."

"And my cousin du Chesne?"

"Du Chesne will be Governor-General of New France, and subdue the Iroquois and discover new countries for the King," said Diane, with a momentary stirring of impatience, quick and vital.

CHAPTER XVII.

THE MATSHI SKOUÉOU.

AS the party came out into the street the flambeaux of the servants flared wildly against the solemn sky of night.

"It is against the rules of the Church, this expedition," hazarded Lydia, raising the most beauteous of anxious eyes.

"Then risk it not," counselled Madame de St. Rochs, briskly. "There is always a danger of being attacked by the savages, but we shall be well protected. For us, that promenade takes place tomorrow. Just fancy, a witch who talks to the devil face to face! It is assuredly a sin, but we will do ample penance afterwards, and Father Denys is never severe to those who are contrite for their sins."

"There is but evil to be found with the witch of the woods and all others of her tribe, I answer to you for that, Mesdames and Messieurs." Bras de Fer removed the pipe from his mouth and gazed around reflectively at the circle of eager faces. Here, where he could pose as an authority, he found no difficulty in expressing his views. "Trust to the experience of a coureur de bois to whom the silence of the forest has taught much that is not found in books. Tales of the most exciting I could tell you of the Lady of the Iris, whom the redskins call Matshi Skouéou."

"Tell us, then, I pray thee, good Baptiste," implored Madame de St. Rochs. "It is in such tales we delight."

"The Matshi Skouéou," the voyageur began, "is in alliance with the Evil One, and this witch must be one of her disciples. Her green eyes possess the power of fascination, like those of a snake. On her head she wears a crown of iris flowers, and she is surrounded by flames of fire. She never appears in the light of day, but at midnight she descends upon a moonbeam, and appears in the foam of waterfalls, in the shadow of dark rocks, or among the mists rising in the valleys. Her favorite hour is when all nature reposes, the time when the fire-flies, those spirits of the lost, dance over the rank marshes; when bats beat the air with their wings, or cling with sharp, slim claws to the rocks; when the silence is broken only by the croaking of frogs and the hou-hou of night birds. It is then the Matshi Skouéou descends to gather the iris with which to crown herself and to invoke the great Manitou.

"'Children,' say the old people, and they know that of which they speak, those old ones; 'never go near the river by moonlight. Hidden behind the rushes the Lady of the Iris watches for her prey; her voice enthralls the senses, but those upon whom her glance falls are blighted. Woe to him who falls into her power.' No, no, Mesdames and Messieurs, remain at home and say your prayers; think not of the witch of the woods."

This salutary advice, instead of allaying the young people's curiosity, served only to increase it. Baptiste, much against his better judgment, was forced to serve as guide to the expedition, and the hardy voyageur uttered the most doleful predictions concerning the disasters that would surely follow this traffic with unholy things.

Far in the heart of the forest stood the solitary lodge of the Witch of the Woods. The witch herself was a diminutive old crone, wrinkled and shrivelled like a mummy, in whom the whole force of a vigorous vitality was gathered in a pair of luminous dark eyes. Displaying no surprise at the late hour which the strangers had chosen for their visit, she received them with cringing servility, the chief characteristic of her face being a kind of animal cunning.

When the merry party found themselves in direct contact with the consequences of their indiscretion, all the fun of the enterprise faded away, and only the undefined sense of terror and mystery remained. In those days superstition reigned supreme; but at the same time existence was environed with real dangers of so many kinds that it required no effort of imagination to create phantoms of dread. As they stood silently seeking mutual support and encouragement amidst the quiet of the forest, a vague sound made itself heard. At first it was scarcely perceptible, but growing more distinct, it rose in waves of tender harmony, and then receded to die away in the distance. Lydia, frightened and tired, began to cry. Bras de Fer had drawn his rosary from his pocket, and was telling over his beads assiduously.

" The blessed saints will bear me witness that I am here against my will," he protested. " Besides that I am protected by a scapulary and a piece of consecrated palm against the attacks of evil spirits."

As the mysterious sounds were resumed, the bushranger looked up gravely from his prayers.

"Ah! well, Mesdames and Messieurs, will you now believe the word of a man who has not gained his knowledge from books? Midnight, the first night of the new moon, that unearthly music! *Voilà!*"

" Bah! that is a seal on the rocks far in the distance," responded du Chesne promptly.

" *Mon dieu!* I fear—I would I had not ventured—I dare not!" Madame de St. Rochs turned her troubled childish face towards her companions, her brown eyes moist with tears, when informed that those who would penetrate the mysteries of futurity must, one by one, accompany the witch into still deeper recesses of the forest. Du Chesne jestingly assured her that as matron of the party she should set an example of dignified courage.

" Let us return, Cecile," proposed her husband.

Young as he was, Armand de St. Rochs had already given incontestible proofs of gallantry, but he had no taste for ghostly terrors and would have avoided them. But the girl-wife's curiosity still exceeded her fear ; she would not consent to abandon her project.

"*Parbleu!* that is demanding too much of a lady. It is the gentlemen's place to lead the way," proposed Crisasi. "I shall be charmed to venture first. Having little to risk and much to hope—."

"And being, as your friends are well aware, a stranger to fear," interrupted du Chesne, laying his hand upon his companion's shoulder in a friendly persuasive fashion.

When after an interval the Chevalier returned to the party his smile was as suave, his tone as bland as usual. No one would have divined that the Sicilian had received, and accepted as irrevocable, his death-warrant. Toward Diane he had gained a new confidence ; his manner was respectful, as became a gentleman, but he scarcely withdrew his eyes from her face. The miserable past and doubtful future were forgotten in the rich flavor of the exquisite present, intensified now by the conviction of its brief duration.

Du Chesne presently reappeared, looking flushed and annoyed.

"It is a cheat ! I saw nothing—but the water was red as blood," he announced.

"*Mort diable!* I am convinced that no deception exists." D'Ordieux shook his perfumed locks excitedly. "I have had the very happiest predictions, far exceeding my expectations, which should naturally be great in a man of my rank—the promise of realizing my dearest hopes. I entertain no doubt of its truth."

"I wish we had not been tempted to come. I shall vow a taper to the Virgin to keep us from harm," whispered Madame de St. Rochs to her husband.

"I am persuaded that this is very wicked. I was induced to consent against my sense of right," murmured Lydia, her blue eyes swimming in tears. She was so deliciously timid and gentle that in his efforts to reassure her du Chesne was betrayed into several trifling follies; but her scruples were not sufficiently urgent to induce her to relinquish her intentions, and she returned from the interview radiant and flushed.

It had finally come to Diane's turn. The shade of the trees was excessively dense, and for an instant the French girl stood confused by the prevailing obscurity and the air of unreality in which all things seemed to be wrapped. Presently she perceived the witch, with a long wand in her hand, standing before a fountain of water. She was speaking rapidly in her native tongue, her voice rising and falling in a weird, monotonous recitative, a strange fantastic incantation in which distant voices appeared to join, rendered more impressive by the perfect stillness of the forest. She could hear sounding and re-echoing a slow, solemn chant, dreamy and plaintive, redolent of mystery and melancholy—long-drawn sighs, the whisper of angels' voices, the song of the winds, all those magical accents that captivate imagination. Then there was a change. Quick and bright came broken

notes, rising to a mad, reckless gaiety that set the
blood aflame ; then mournful melody like the autumn
wind moaning in the branches, deepening and still
deepening ; anon rising into the flourish of trumpets
on the battle-field, and ending in a funeral hymn
floating through the dim aisles of some vast cathe-
dral.   It was like the entrance into dream-life, for
those enchanted strains embodied all the extremes of
human joy and suffering, aspiration and yearning.

As she listened, the witch's decrepit form expanded,
acquiring size, height and dignity ; the crafty, sensual
features gained a strange power and majesty.   A
sudden sense of mystery, of dominant and all but
overpowering force, took possession of Diane.   Every
thought of her heart, to the very depth of her being,
seemed familiar to this influence and responsive to its
command.   She shivered with an excited desperation
of feeling, of mingled desire and apprehension, of
attraction and repulsion.   A rich, heavy perfume,
resembling the fragrance of incense, filled the air, and
a thick cloud hung over the large basin of water
which stood before her.   Obeying an imperious gesture of the Indian woman, the girl advanced and bent
over the basin.

Diane's form grew rigid as she stood with eyes
fixed on the water, their pupils dilated in a terror-
stricken gaze.   A light film of pungent smoke arose,
which, wreathing itself in airy circles, seemed to catch
a fiery color from some unseen flame.   Then, gradually crystallizing, it assumed definite form.   Was it

a tissue of fancy and reality that produced a creation
so fantastic? Vaguely, as in a dream, she perceived
remote vistas, all weird and mysterious, peopled by
spectral shapes, resounding with far-off, uncertain
footsteps. Then out of the darkness there glided
wavering, shadowy figures, at first faint and indefinite,
then gradually becoming more distinct. Clear as a
reflection in a mirror, every trifling, delicate detail
perceptible, the scene shaped itself before her eager
gaze. It was a spacious apartment; two nuns were
moving softly to and fro about the lofty four-post
bed; wax tapers, in tall curiously-chased silver can-
dlesticks, shed a softened radiance upon the room.
Lying on the bed, still and stately, like the heroic
statue of some knight asleep upon his tomb, lay a
young man. In the shadow a girl, slender and delicately formed, knelt upon a *prie-dieu*, her head bowed
upon her tightly clasped hands. For a time she
seemed to be looking on some scene that she had
long known and loved, but which had taken on a
new aspect. Then as the flickering, uncertain light
settled into a clearer reflection, Mademoiselle de
Monesthrol asked herself if that aged nun with the
sweet, benign expression did not surely resemble the
venerable Sister Marguerite Bourgeois; and that
other, taller and more active, certainly must be
Sister Berbier, Superior of the Congregation of
Notre Dame. The young man's features were concealed from her, but the girlish mourner moved, and
with the listlessness of apathetic suffering turned her
head.

A horrible paralyzing dread ran shuddering through Diane's veins, for that face, haggard, bloodless, convulsed by inexpressible grief, was her own. Then a thick cloud of darkness passed between her and the mystic scene; she was conscious only that the glowing eyes of the witch were riveted intensely upon her. When, bewildered, she turned to look again, all had collapsed like shadows in a dream; the basin of water alone remained.

Diane did not often lose self-command. In this supreme crisis, when all things seemed to be slipping away from her, she fought to persuade herself that what she had seen had been all a creation of her own imagination. A faint smile, like the palest of winter sunshine, curved her lips; her hands tightened in a silent struggle at self-restraint. When she raised her white face, a proud, confident look shone from her eyes.

"Never yet has it been in the power of danger and disaster to daunt the spirit of a de Monesthrol. Others have suffered—I may suffer—yet are we still in the hands of the good God." Drawing herself up with conscious dignity, Diane spoke as though hurling defiance at some unknown and threatening power.

The soft sounds of quivering leaves were the only noises that disturbed the silence of the forest; she seemed to be surrounded by darkling shadows profound with fate. The witch crouched low on the ground, her face hidden in the folds of her blanket.

"We have been guilty of a folly. It is but an idle jest," Diane said quietly as she rejoined her companions. "We can go home now and do penance for the sin we have committed."

"Now that it is over I do not care about our expedition in the least," grumbled Madame de St. Rochs, who was tired and sleepy, and who had not received the flattering predictions which her youthful buoyancy of spirit had led her to anticipate.

Crisasi regarded Mademoiselle de Monesthrol earnestly. The man who loved her alone perceived that the girl was stricken, and that, with hand clenched hard against her heart, she was resolutely striving to control her throbbing pulses.

"It has, indeed, been tiresome, and not worth the trouble," he said gently.

In the serene composure of Diane's outward bearing as she left the scene there was no trace of the tense passion and misery that were gnawing at her heart. She was resolved calmly to face the future, whatever it might contain.

That night, as the French girl lay awake, a strange flash of realization came over her. Panting with pain and terror, flinging up her hands in the darkness, she cried desperately :

"Holy Virgin! deliver me. That which I never imagined has come upon me—has conquered me— that which will never again leave me in peace, all my life long. Something beautiful and terrible—so terrible! Holy Virgin! thou hast a woman's heart— deliver me from this!"

CHAPTER XVIII.

SAINTLY PROTECTION.

WITH each returning morn the land awoke, glad and fragrant, at the caress of the pale dawn. The rooks clamored in their nests, the fish rose in the lazy streams, the robins sang plaintively among the shrubs. Mount Royal, St. Helen's Island and the St. Lawrence glowed palpitant in the magical summer haze. All nature seemed to breathe a spirit of tranquil peace.

But despite this calm a dark cloud of alarm hung over the colony. The air was full of rumors concerning the expedition which it was confidently alleged the English were about to direct against Canada. Priests and traders, nobles and bourgeois, bushrangers, and red-skinned children of the forest, were content to forget prejudices and animosities in consideration of the common interest, and to unite in the extremity of their peril. Yet through all, the elements of true Gallic light-heartedness relieved the poignant distress of the moment.

It was plainly understood that the situation of the colony was most precarious. The garrison of Ville

Marie consisted of but seven or eight hundred soldiers, and of these many were posted at various points in the surrounding country to protect the colonists while gathering in the harvest. It was deemed advisable to draw in all of these for the protection of the town. Prolonged echoes reverberated from Mount Royal and across the St. Lawrence as guns were fired to recall the troops. Soon they began to arrive, accompanied by many of the settlers seeking the protection of the forts.

At this crisis the clamor of fear and anxiety and endeavor penetrated even to the cloistered cell where the recluse, Jeanne Le Ber, strove to shut out all sign of earth's joys and sorrows, and to devote herself to the contemplation of heavenly glories. Yielding to the urgent entreaties of the Sisters of the Congregation, Jeanne Le Ber wrote upon a sacred picture a prayer of her own composing, addressed to the Virgin. This the nuns caused to be fastened up on a barn in the country (owned by the community, and supposed to be peculiarly liable to attack), as a sort of talisman, to preserve it from harm. This was Anne Barroy's hour of triumph; enjoying it to the fullest extent, her pride swelled to enormous proportions. At this moment beauty, birth, breeding and worldly pride could bear no comparison with the temporal as well as spiritual advantages of superior holiness. "Our saint" and "that sainted one" were the mildest terms in which Anne permitted herself to allude to her cousin, and she never wearied of talking.

"When I enter her apartment," the enthusiast would declare, with impressive solemnity, "I perceive in the air a certain odor of sanctity which gives me the sensation of an agreeable perfume. Truly she speaks like a seraph and is the companion of angels. What a blessing to rest beneath a roof which affords shelter to so perfect a creature, though there may be those not so far away who fail to appreciate their privileges."

"For me!" cried Nanon with a clatter, "I had no necessity to travel to Canada to make acquaintance with saints. We have them at home, and of superior quality. There was St. Anne d'Auray, Mother of the Blessed Virgin; and St. Geneviève of Paris, at whose shrine kings and nobles worshipped; but indeed, I have no taste for home-made articles."

Anne continued as though she were not aware of the interruption. She knew that at this moment her words were eagerly listened to.

"Indeed, our saint accumulates merits against the day of judgment; those who are wise would strive to share a small portion of them. From her earliest years she began the study of perfection; every virtue was seen and admired in her. It is the country of saints, this. Behold the head of the martyred Frenchman, which amazed the Iroquois who had cut it off by scolding them roundly for their perfidy, and threatening them with the vengeance of Heaven. Think, also, of the handkerchief of the late Père la Maitre (may his soul rest in Paradise!) stamped indelibly, as on a piece of wax, with the features of its former owner. The heathen Iroquois have ever since been seen using it as a banner in battle. Should the country be saved, our deliverance will be due to the prayers of our sainted one, who has sacrificed herself as an expiatory offering for Canada."

"Might I commend myself to the good prayers of our reverend demoiselle, and particularly to the sacrifice of the Mass for my intention," urged Jean Ameron, with eager subserviency. "And are you quite persuaded, Mam'selle Anne, that our saint's credit with the powers of heaven will be sufficient to protect Canada from those sorcerers of English?"

Nanon glared at her adorer, who had so readily gone over to the enemy, but in his fright his mistress' ire had no terror for Jean. Anne hastened to reassure him.

"Certainly. Have not the gentlemen of the Seminary and the blessed Sisters of the Congregation of Notre Dame given ready testimony to her perfection? Can you doubt the power of the saints, given them by the blessed Virgin herself?"

"Assuredly not, nor should I dare to presume. Without doubt it is a convenience to find one's self near a holy saint, if she will but remember the needs of the poor sinners, and exert her credit with all the heavenly host on our account. Could our sainted demoiselle be persuaded but to write me a little word that I might wear with my scapulary to perserve me from evil fortune? *Voilà*, Mam'selle Anne, if you would have the goodness to remark the fact, like the demoiselle Le Ber herself I have denied myself the happiness of matrimony in order to merit the favor of Heaven."

"Ta, ta! there are saints and saints, my son, and thou wouldst place thyself among them. Wilt thou then dare to compare thyself to that spotless creature, reverenced by all the world for her holiness, who is an expiatory offering for the sins of her country, and not a refuge for cowardly lackeys? Out of my presence! It is that unruly ostrich Nanon who has inspired thee with the thought of such impertinence!" cried Anne with growing fury.

"Mam'selle Anne has always reason. Yet doubtless you will allow that my bones are precious to me, and that it is a duty to take thought for one's self," whimpered Jean.

When Jeanne Le Ber's prayer disappeared, stolen from the edifice to which it had been attached, to the consternation of the good Sisters who had trusted implicitly in its efficacy, no one suspected the immense solace which Jean derived from having it tucked comfortably away under his scapulary.

CHAPTER XIX.

A WOMAN'S LOYALTY.

ONE day scouts coming into the town informed the Military Governor, M. de Callière, that Peter Schuyler, with a strong force of English and Dutch troops, accompanied by Mohawks, Wolves and Mohegans, was marching on Ville Marie. Rumor magnified the actual facts to the most exaggerated proportions. A crowd of anxious people blocked the streets in every direction.

"Is it true that the invaders are close at hand?" asked the baker.

"But assuredly," responded the grocer, who in his haste had forgotten to remove his blue woollen nightcap, the corner of which dangled rakishly over his left eye. "It is the English who will make mincemeat of us. They have sold themselves to the devil, and bathe themselves in the blood of little children. I already see us all being devoured."

"Ah! my good St. Anne!" cried a young woman, whose short homespun skirt revealed a trim pair of ankles. "Can anyone tell if they are numerous, these sorcerers of English?"

"Numerous, good woman? *Dame!* but like the

sands of the sea. A thousand fire-eaters are close at hand." A soldier who happened to be passing amused himself at the public expense.

"Javotte! Javotte!" the woman shrieked, waving her hands excitedly. "Five thousand English are upon us ; we are all to be scalped and taken prisoners immediately!"

This terrifying prediction spread among the populace, creating consternation which almost amounted to a panic. Meanwhile energetic preparations for defence were being made. All the military and most of the bourgeois were under arms ; among the soldiers appeared old men and young lads who, in ordinary cases, would have been considered unfit for service. It had become an absolute necessity that anyone who could shoulder a musket should lend a helping hand. Women and children, who at the signal of alarm had come in from the surrounding country, were busily occupied in carrying their poor possessions to the shelter of the citadel or to the convents. Here an invalid with pale face was carried on a hastily improvised stretcher ; there an old man, anxious to preserve the poor remnant of life that remained to him, tottered feebly, leaning on his daughter's arm ; yonder a young mother, frantic with terror, flying in search of refuge, bore in her arms a tiny babe, the little one regarding with true infantile calmness the unfamiliar scene of tumult and confusion.

"Make way there, good people, make way!" cried a stout, robust woman, who was bearing a large blue wooden chest, into which she had thrown pell-mell everything she could collect—clothing, furniture and cooking utensils all huddled together—and which was so heavy that it seemed a marvel she could move it at all. "It is hard enough to get along with never a man's hand to help, or even to push, without being blocked up as well. Make way there, I say!"

"Make way then yourself, Pétronille," retorted the sharp, quivering voice of a tiny, withered old crone, staggering under the weight of a feather-bed. "Chut! screech-owl! see to it."

"*Allons!* Mère Poisson, bite with but one tooth. Rest tranquil, I pray you. At your age it would appear more seemly to rest upon your mattress than to drag it about the streets in the open light of day."

"And your rubbish had better be burnt, it is so long since those things have touched water."

The shrewish Pétronille, enraged by the taunt, roughly jostled her neighbor, who fell against a child carrying a clock; the glass cracked into splinters, while a nail, standing out from the chest, tore a hole in the covering of the mattress, from which the feathers escaped, flying out in a cloud. The child cried, the old woman loudly lamented the catastrophe, but Pétronille, without even turning her head, and still dragging her chest, pushed her way resolutely on.

It was decided by the authorities that M. de Callière should encamp at La Prairie, to be in readiness to meet Schuyler's attack, while Valrenne, an officer of birth and ability, should proceed to Chambly with one hundred and sixty regulars and Canadians, a body of Huron and Algonquin converts, and another band of Algonquin converts from the Ottawa, in order to intercept any of the English forces which might chance to come by that way.

"Du Chesne goes in command of the Canadians." Jacques Le Ber spoke with a long-drawn sigh, that seemed to come from the depths of his heart. These tragic episodes were interruptions to his own serious interests. More than that, affection for his youngest son was entwined with the closest fibres of his nature, and no one recognized the dangers of forest warfare more clearly than the grave merchant, experienced in such strife, who himself had ever been ready to serve his country.

"They are going to lay siege to Paradise, to win it and enter in, because they are fighting for religion and the faith." A sort of passionate insistence contrasted oddly with the ordinary calm preciseness of Pierre Le Ber's level tones. The words fell upon the father's ear like a prediction which he resented. He regarded his eldest son with a mingling of reverence and impatience, and then turned to seek comfort in Diane de Monesthrol's open, steadfast gaze.

"It is but a plain duty, my uncle; a soldier belongs to his country. It is an honor that du Chesne should have been selected. The men adore him; there is no one who has as much influence with them as he. How proud we all shall be when he returns covered with glory." The liquid voice, speaking in tones of deepest compassion and tenderness, penetrated to the core of the man's scheming, worldly nature.

"Certainly times may change, my rabbit. Before now we have been reduced to extremities, and have found deliverance. It may happen so again. Whichever way it goes, there is nothing to be done but make the best of it." Saying this, Le Ber shrugged his shoulders with resigned emphasis, though there were strange nervous twitches about his firm lips.

Diane was so young, so buoyant in her hopes, so high-spirited and high-hearted, that neither fear nor shadow of disaster could easily crush her. This was a time of trial, to be lived through as best they could, but it seemed positive that, after all, things must go well. With the sweet agitation of hope and delight dancing in her veins, she felt only elation from the excitement around her. The spectacle of a courage absolutely free from egotism was too common among the devoted Canadian women of the day to attract much attention. Yet it was with some surprise that those about saw Mademoiselle de Monesthrol throwing off the dainty air of stateliness which was considered becoming to her station, and growing sweet and womanly in the glory of self-sacrifice. It was difficult to identify the proud and capricious beauty with the gentle girl whose watchful eye and helpful hand were at the service of all, who in a frank, generous fashion dealt out cheer and sympathy to whoever chanced to need it.

"This is a change I scarcely expected, a new development," mused the Marquise, always critical and philosophical. "Well, the little one comes of a race born brave and generous." For an instant the keen eyes softened, the delicate features quivered, as warm waves of memory rolled over the proud woman's soul.

"Diane, I must talk with you. I can trust you entirely." Du Chesne spoke eagerly.

A hot wave of color swept over the girl's face, but she raised her eyes frankly to the young man's.

Out of the careless gladness of his youth du Chesne was going forth to meet the solemn future, full of lights and shadows. Nature breathed into his heart an inarticulate thrill of prophecy, a dark foreboding. He paused before advancing lightly to meet that fate, whatever it might be. Grasping the outstretched slender hands so hard that the pressure hurt the girl, he gazed at her with a subdued and silent tenderness, such as he might bestow upon a sister. There was a shadow of anxious care upon the merry, boyish face which no one could ever have associated with du Chesne. He sought assurance and comfort from the companion of his childhood. As he watched the moist red lips close firm and sweet above the delicate chin, he was persuaded that his expectation would not be disappointed. With a sob of excitement and agitation swelling in her throat, Diane returned his gaze. A cry of momentary anguish almost escaped her, but she scorned herself for the failure of courage, and forced a smile upon lips that quivered. It was not weak repining, but encouragement to strengthen his heart in time of need, that a man had the right to expect from the woman who loved him.

" I have had too much experience of forest warfare not to know that I take my life—aye, and carry it lightly, too—in my hand. A stray shot from behind a tree"—Diane shivered—" a random blow from a tomahawk, and all is over. There are things I would settle in case an accident should befall me. I know you will be a true daughter to my father, who loves you as though you were his own. And for Pierre— our good Pierre," knitting his brows in perplexity over a problem to which he had failed to find a solution, " I don't know. Things arrange themselves, Diane ; don't trifle with him, or lose heart, my dear. I have promised a mass in honor of the good St. Anne that things may go well with you both, though I know not how. You have never trusted me as I mean to trust you."

Diane's heart suddenly stilled its fluttering, and sank like lead. Of what interest at this supreme moment were Pierre's concerns that they should be allowed to occupy word or thought.

"We have been as brother and sister, truly attached,—is it not so, Diane? I can remember now exactly what you looked like when my father arrived

holding you in his arms, saying that you would be
my little companion, and that I must be gentle and
learn to protect you; and I was so proud to have a
little lady for my playmate. You have, indeed, been
a sunbeam in our house. Before we part I would
share my secret with you, knowing I can rely upon
your sympathy."

The conscious face, with its hot color and drooping
eyes; the air of happy confusion that sat so curiously
upon impetuous, light-hearted du Chesne; the tenderness that softened the force and boldness of his
features, thrilled the girl who stood beside him.

"On my return I shall ask my father's consent to
make Lydia my wife. Should success attend our
arms it will be a propitious moment to win a hearing,
and I want you to use your influence, which is great,
to plead my cause. My father is ambitious; greatly
as he is attached to me, I am by no means certain
that his sanction will be easily gained. From the
first moment that my eyes rested upon the English
captive I have loved her. All through the winter
before I met her I had passed through toil and
danger and carnage, and then that summer day her
tender presence dawned upon me like some star of
peace and repose. You, too, have been won by her
sweetness. It was together we rescued her, remember, Diane. I never loved you so dearly as when I
watched your tender care of the helpless stranger cast
upon your mercy. She has the gift of winning all
hearts. For my sake I would ask you to protect and
care for my treasure."

Du Chesne was so completely engrossed by his own thoughts and feelings that he paid but slight attention to his companion. Diane's rich color had given place to a strange excited pallor. She looked at him with the wild, hunted eyes of some desperate animal at bay. The world was suddenly upheaving beneath her feet, and her heart stood still as the keenness and sharpness of the shock crushed the spirit within her.

Oh, Heaven! not later than yesterday she had been as a queen, graciously dispensing her favors, smiling tolerantly at Lydia's petty vanities and weaknesses—Lydia, who had come into her life as a stranger, stirring it to its very foundations, robbing it of peace and happiness, leaving her in return the blank of a great desolation—Lydia, whom she had protected and cherished, who owed all to her generosity. Now a flash of lightning had come out of the apparently cloudless sky, smiting her from her pedestal, precipitating her into this awful void in which every wretchedness was conceivable. Others had not been as blind as herself. She remembered her aunt's sarcasm, the hints Nanon had given her, the ill-will to the English girl Cecile de St. Rochs had so often openly expressed. The glare of illumination was intolerable, bringing with it a galling, insupportable mortification. As these bitter truths flashed upon her, Diane clenched her hands, flushing into a sudden rage of bitter humiliation.

"Diane, you are surely not surprised? I thought

that you, who are so quick, would have divined my feeling from the first. I fancied that your kindness to Lydia was inspired by friendship for me, as well as delight in her charms."

The trustful glance of the young man's frank, eager eyes melted the fire of pain and rage and jealousy. A piteous little smile crossed her lips, as though she were amused at, yet very sorry for, that proud, high-handed girl who had fancied herself supreme, and who was none other than her old self. The vehement, hot-blooded creature was overwhelmed by a black pall of shame and self-disgust. What did it matter if the whole world crumbled away, and that her pride and vanity vanished with it? If du Chesne sought comfort it must be her place, crowned by the glory and agony of self-sacrifice, to supply it. No one could supplant the companion of his childhood in that office. Turning her resolute face to the future, without wasting a single thought upon her own strength or need, she battled against the rush of strong feeling with a fierce, determined energy.

Diane could scarcely stand, but she confronted the young Canadian with a brave smile, a dumb denial of her anguish, and even succeeded in assuming an air of gaiety.

"You did take me by surprise. I had no thought of this. But I am grateful for your confidence, and shall try to prove myself worthy. And then, my cousin, when you return——"

" Aye, return, who can tell how that will be."

He paled before a supposition to which he dreaded to give form even in his thoughts. Together with a stern sense of his own immediate duty, which was to put through the work in hand steadily and cheerfully, without any careful hesitation or speculation concerning the ultimate ethics of the situation, there existed in Le Ber's youngest son much tenderness of heart towards the weak and unfortunate, and delicate consideration for friends and kindred, as well as ardent devotion to the chosen one of his heart. Existence was full of hope and generous ambition; he was surrounded by kindly, faithful faces and honest love. In the strength of his early manhood he was conscious of stirring hopes and untold possibilities, above which shone the thought of his girl-love with her innocent grace and guilelessness. All this was deepened by that touch of uncertainty that gives exquisite intensity to affection, and the quickened interest of tragic possibilities. These fancies were followed by wiser and sadder thoughts, and immediate practical considerations. Just as the color grew richer and the pace faster, and life spread before him a full completeness he had never even imagined, was it, he asked himself, to be stained forever by the cruelty of circumstances? A great wave of sadness, a swift dread of advancing pain and disaster, the reaction from his natural buoyancy of temperament, rushed over du Chesne's spirit.

"Somehow, Diane, when I try to picture my return, I cannot imagine how it will be. Many times before

have I started on such expeditions without a thought;
this time it is entirely different. I cannot help re-
membering—it was less than a year ago—St. Helène's
fate. Then De Clermont, Bienville, De Bellefonds,
De la Motte, were close friends and trusty comrades,
with whom I fought and camped and hunted; where
are they? Gallant gentlemen, they have laid down
their lives, gaily and carelessly, for King and country.
Mort dieu! what will you? A day sooner or later
makes but little difference. Shall I make a nightmare of death?"

One thing, evident and definite, seemed to clear
Diane's dazzled senses—du Chesne had turned to her
for comfort. She held his hand with a strong com-
pelling pressure which had in it no trace of selfish
sentiment.

"But there are others, my cousin, whose duty
compels them constantly to go upon such expeditions, and who have ever returned unharmed."

"Yes, but to you I do not mind confessing that for
the last few days I have been unnerved by strange
fancies. It is because another's fate depends upon
my own. It is for her, so young, so tender and
trusting, without protection of friend or relative; at
this thought the heart melts within me, and there is
nothing to be done. Diane, you have ever been
strong and true; you could not fail one who trusts
you."

The strength of one dedicated to a pure and elevated purpose flamed into Mademoiselle de Mones-

throl's eyes; all her face grew nobly luminous. Every word she spoke was crystal clear, coming straight from the heart.

"You can trust me, du Chesne. I will be to Lydia a loving sister; I will place her welfare before my own. With our Blessed Lady's help I will be as true and tender to her as I would be to you."

"In life or death I commit her to your charge. You have removed my heaviest care." Du Chesne bent reverently to kiss the warm hand that clasped his own. "I shall have perfect peace in trusting to the loyalty of my brave and tender sister."

CHAPTER XX.

PREPARING FOR THE EXPEDITION.

PIERRE LE BER had lately been occupied in painting upon a piece of fair white linen a picture of the Virgin, and this he had embellished with all the beauties which an ardent imagination could suggest.

"*Ciel!*" cried Nanon, regarding the painting attentively, "It is a beautiful picture, and in truth it resembles our demoiselle."

This speech greatly scandalized Anne Barroy.

"It is not sufficient that this proud turkey would claim for her mistress highest rank on earth; she would fain push her to the front among the heavenly host as well," she whispered to one of her familiars.

Jeanne Le Ber, who excelled in embroidery, had made a very beautiful banner for the picture, and it was decided that this emblem of the protectress of the settlement should be presented to the war-party as a safeguard. Recognizing the fact that the panic-stricken settlers required every available encouragement that could be derived from both faith and patriotism, the ecclesiastical authorities organized a procession, as imposing as the resources of the colony would allow, to carry the flag to the Parish Church of Notre Dame, where it was to be consecrated by Dollier de Casson.

The church was a spacious building. Above the great altar, blazing with lights, rose an immense wooden image of our Saviour suspended on the cross. Behind it the dim glories of the choir deepened into golden gloom. From the lofty rood screen dark shadows, thrown by the lights of distant altars, brooded over the space beyond. At the head of the church, near the chancel, was placed a *prie-dieu* for the Governor of Ville Marie, who was surrounded by a brilliant group of officers. Soldiers thronged the side aisles, and all the intervening space was occupied by the confused movement of the throng of spectators. The eager faces of all turned toward the high altar, with the banner displayed before it, as though therein lay their only hope. Wistful women, scarcely able to restrain their streaming tears, or wrapt in the heroism of some higher purpose, gazed, hushed and awed, upon the little band of heroes who for faith and country were willing to face danger and risk life itself. Tears came to haggard eyes looking upon the flag. Patriotism was an inspiring principle, faith a fervent flame, to those who had already made great sacrifices for religion and country ; there was even a thrill of sweetness in the thought of dying for it. A fine and simple courage sustained many a sinking spirit, and in the contagion of popular enthusiasm there was but slight betrayal of individual weakness.

Many were moved to an almost passionate exhilaration by the martial music, while others were overcome by the pathos of the brave show, with its implied possibilities of horror, agony and death.

The service proceeded with intoning of litanies and chanting of psalms. From a grated gallery, beyond the obscurity of the screen and crucifix, floated the delicate harmony of sweet voices in wave after wave of soft melody, like the measured refrain of an angelic choir, echoes of an eternal voice speaking to the human soul. The choir intoned the *libera*, and when the concluding words of the last verse died away in the arched roof, a woman's voice, clear, pure and penetratingly sweet, arose in the *miseremine* :

"*Miseremine mei, miseremine mei saltem vos amici mei. De profundis clamavi ad te, Domine, Domine exaudi vocem meam.*"

In the deepness of her human anguish, from the longing for strength to sustain a wounded spirit and fainting flesh, Diane de Monesthrol repeated :

"Out of the depths I cry unto Thee, oh, my God ! "

She had come to realize that for herself nothing remained but an absolute, solitary and sorrowful renunciation ; but this was no time for indulgence in sinking of heart or depression of soul. Some spirit stronger than herself took hold of her, giving her the look of an embodied passion, beautiful but terrible. Her figure and her whole attitude were instinct with resolution ; every word and movement was vitalized by an inspiration. Her face was full of vehement life—eyes kindling, cheeks flushed, lips trembling, nostrils quivering. Led by some subtle intuition, timid souls crept near her for comfort and support. If an impatient expression broke from her unawares, she quickly controlled herself, and followed it with words of hope and consolation. Suffering was so new to her that any sort of exertion seemed preferable to passive endurance.

"Don't leave me, Diane; you inspire me with courage. Oh! it is fine to be brave and strong as you; but then you are not risking your heart's dearest; and you, who laugh at men's follies, and despise their sentiment, you have never known what it is to give your heart to one alone. Hold me fast, then, Diane; let me feel you close when the time comes to look my last on Armand's face—perhaps for ever. Oh! I dare not allow myself to think of that possibility. I am a soldier's wife; do not let me forget it. I promised him to be brave, though my heart should break with the effort; he must not see me fail," whispered little Madame de St. Rochs, all her childish features quivering in the effort to restrain her grief.

"My Cecile, your gallant soldier may be proud of your courage. You will do your best to strengthen his heart."

An old woman, with two weeping children clutching frantically at the skirts of her gown, paused in mumbling her rosary as Diane passed, and held up her withered hands imploringly.

"Oh, Mademoiselle! it is Pierrot, my youngest, the father of these helpless little ones, who goes with the expedition. Their mother died at Easter. If anything happens to him they have but me to look to; and in these expeditions each man has his share, big or little, according to the size of the cake—"

"It is to fight for his country, my poor Mère Bernichou."

"His country—but yes, they all say their skin belongs to themselves, and they must dispose of it to their taste; but when the men are killed what is to become of the old people and the babies, I ask you that? Three of Pierrot's brothers went the same way, but not one ever returned. He is as strong as a lion, and he worked for us so well. Oh, my good and noble demoiselle! you are of those who are listened to by the Blessed Virgin and the holy saints; pray for us, I implore you."

Lydia, the tears running down her pretty, piteous face, with so sad a curve of lips that seemed made for smiles, so wistful a glance in the swimming blue eyes, made no effort to control her sorrowful consternation. Trembling and shivering she clung to her friend's arm, and Diane was able to soothe her as a generous woman in her tribulation may seek to console a creature more dependent than herself. She could even keep in mind the fact that, though weak and frivolous, Lydia had proved herself neither base nor deliberately treacherous; and she tried loyally to remember that in every kindness she offered the English girl she was lightening du Chesne's burden.

As the crowd surged out from the church and flocked down to the beach, the scene was a bright and varied one. The St. Lawrence stretched out like a great mirror under the blaze of sunshine, reflecting every floating cloud above. St. Helen's, with banks of velvet softness, arose out of this liquid light; the Mountain was varied with a hundred restless rays playing upon secluded slopes and woody hollows. The summer sun gleamed brightly upon bayonets and naked swords, and shone on the rich costumes of the gallant French officers, whose nodding plumes shaded hats adorned with gold, and whose lace ruffles, sashes and sword-knots made a brave show. Some of the regulars wore light armor, while the Canadians were in plain attire of coarse cloth and buckskin, their provisions strapped on their backs. Much rivalry existed between the latter and the French. The Canadians had adopted the Indian mode of fighting, while the Frenchmen, accustomed only to civilized warfare, found it difficult to adapt themselves to the methods of the savages.

Among the soldiers walked, with a solemn dignity befitting the occasion, the dog which was inscribed on the regimental list as M. de Niagara, and to whom regular rations were granted. The progeny of a dog named Vingt Sols, who had done good service at the fort of Niagara, where he was held in high esteem, this animal had been brought from that place by M. de Bergères and taken to Chambly, where his master served as commandant. As the roads leading to this post were often blocked by Iroquois war parties, it was found extremely difficult to send or receive news from Montreal. At this critical juncture M. de Niagara solved the problem of how despatches might be conveyed. It was noticed by the garrison at Chambly that the dog found his way of his own accord to La Prairie de la Madeleine. Fearing that some of the French with whom he had started had been captured by their enemies, a letter was written and fastened to the animal's collar, and he was driven out of the fort. He at once took the road whence he had come· Reaching Chambly, the despatch was read, and, with an answer tied to his collar, the dog was sent off again. Thus communication was established between the two posts, and many a life saved. M. de Niagara always took part in reviews, was profoundly conscious of his own importance, and was regarded by the soldiers with the greatest affection as a true and staunch comrade.

A corporal drummer, escorted by two armed soldiers, marched through the streets beating a rhythmic movement, which, joined with the shrill notes of a fife, thrilled the nerves, while the air resounded with the deep clamor of bells mingling with the fantastic cries of the Indians and bushrangers. The condition of things was so precarious that a courage born of desperation inspired the colonists. " In order to breathe," they assured one another, " one must hope." It was hard to realize grim possibilities of death and disaster amidst sunshine and music and movement. After

all, if the worst were to come, it was better to enjoy
the present moment. The spirit of adventure had
already made itself felt in the French blood, a rapid
current wonderfully susceptible to elation. A wild
gaiety began to exhibit itself. Not to be subdued by
an emergency, certain lively youths could be heard
shouting hilariously to one another.

"I lost my tobacco pouch," cried Bras de Fer, to
whom the prospect of action had restored a com-
fortable spirit of self-assertion; "one quite new, too,
made out of the skin of a little seal that I killed on
the Island of M. de St. Helène last year. Ah! if one
of those English wizards falls into my claws, and I
don't succeed in making a better pouch out of his
skin, may I be scalped before All Saints. The fox
counts on eating the goose, but there are occasions
when things turn the other way; then it is the goose
who gets a chance at the fox. Our hearts are in this
affair, and that is something."

"It is impossible to content all the world and his
father," grumbled an old soldier, "or to take time to
enquire what his servants, his ass or his ox may
think about. For my part, I enjoy these little skirm-
ishes; they give a spice of variety to life. I don't
want to spend my days telling stories in the chimney
corner."

"My little brother Jaquot, a true imp of the devil,
who is only thirteen and can manage the arquebus
like a man, says, 'It's the season for plums, and truly
we will make them eat the stones.' No fear but we

shall turn out all right. Our captain is brave as the
King's sword; no one need fear to follow his lead.
After all, I like better to kill the devil than to permit
him to kill me. But pardon, my commandant,"—
Baptiste took the freedom of an old and trusted servant—"Pardon, but it is an evil day to start on an
expedition."

"And why, pray, Master Bras de Fer? What are
you croaking about there, old bird of ill-omen?" All
shade of melancholy had passed from du Chesne's
spirit as soon as practical affairs required his attention. His face was now all alight with martial excitement. Amidst the cheerful sounds of human bustle
and movement his spirits rose to any height of
adventure.

"Is not to-day Friday? Don't laugh, my commandant; we don't learn these things from books,
they are what we see and know; every chance counts.
The day of ill-omen, I would it were another day we
were starting."

"Bah! old wives' tales," du Chesne laughed merrily.
"You will never give a thought to that when once the
fight begins. Let me hear no more such nonsense."

Bras de Fer shook his head in solemn disap-
probation.

"A closed mouth never swallows flies. I might
have spared my breath. To think that I carried him
in my arms and taught him to shoot! The Lord
send me plenty such commandants, there are not
many like him; but Friday—I like it not."

"You have a rage for searching noon at fourteen o'clock, my poor Bras de Fer," remonstrated the old soldier. "*Saccagé—Chien!* I have heard that spoken of—the ill-luck of starting on Friday—but once let us come in sight of those English and we shall think of neither A nor B."

CHAPTER XXI.

BAPTISTE FINDS HIS WITS.

NANON, who for the last few days had been as restless as an unquiet spirit, had followed her mistress down to the beach, and now stood close at hand, watching the preparations for departure which were being energetically carried on. She found herself in a position antagonistic to all her former instincts. Those about her were so completely engrossed by their own concerns that no one remarked how greatly Nanon had changed in the last few days. The Frenchwoman's rich brown complexion had turned to dark chalk color; her cap, usually poised so coquettishly, was pushed carelessly to the extreme corner of her head; the crushed lappets hung limp over her shoulders, her cheeks had lost their rounded contour, her eyes were red and swollen with crying. A rueful sense of loss was troubling her, and she had even ceased to care whether Anne Barroy suspected the cause of her affliction.

"Is it for her sins that poor Nanon is taking thought, or is it the men who are pleased to go that she is weeping for?" Anne had whispered to a crony, taking care that her voice should be quite loud enough to be overheard.

The malicious words revived Nanon's spirit. As she spoke there was a blaze of fiery agitation, and a light of pain flashed through the moisture in her eyes.

"Yes, it is for the brave men going to their death that I am crying. I am not ashamed of being soft-hearted; if there were more like me it would be to their credit."

"The poor Nanon! she fears that she may be left to make *la tire* on the feast of St. Catharine."*

Baptiste, smoking his pipe in silence, eyed Nanon reflectively. He was very slow, but he was very sure, and an heroic resolve was gradually assuming definite proportions in his mind. Things could not continue as they had been; any change was better than that. He meditated upon his long, hopeless passion. When did it begin? He could not decide that; it seemed always to have dominated him. Away in the forest, amidst toil, hardship and privation, when he thought of home, it was Nanon's saucy face that smiled upon him. He thought upon all the wit and sparkling vivacity that rendered his cruel love charming, the oppressive thraldom in which she had held him, the burning pains of jealousy which he had endured. No one knew better the dangers of an expedition such as that upon which he and his comrades were starting, and none dreaded them less than Baptiste Leroux But the thought that he might never again see Nanon confused and depressed his mind; happily it also

---

*A saying commonly applied to confirmed spinsters.

inspired the great simple fellow with a more desperate courage than any required to resist the attacks of English or Iroquois, or to die in defence of his country.

"That is the last of all trades—a coward," he said to himself. "My principle has always been to conduct matters by beat of drum. After all, I can be in no worse condition than I am now; so here goes, even if I pay through the nose for it."

He stretched out his strong right arm, quietly took possession of his coquettish mistress,—who appeared to be so entirely taken by surprise that she made no attempt to offer resistance—enveloped her in a great bear's hug, kissed her once, twice, a dozen times, then recovering himself, loosened his hold. Realizing the enormity of his offence he stood humbled and contrite, with bowed head, to receive the punishment of his audacity. He could conceive no idea of what form the tempest which was about to break upon his devoted head was to assume, but even the noisiest clamor of Nanon's sharp tongue would be less terrible to bear than this breathless silence. Feeling that he could no longer endure the suspense, he burst out impetuously :

"I do not care, I could not help it; you may be enraged if it pleases you; in truth, I could no longer contain myself. Any good woman would have some pity on a poor fellow." Words were scarce with Bras de Fer, but now he was fairly started, the sound of his own eloquence delighted him, and he continued boldly, " If to-morrow I am to be scalped, or thrown into the Iroquois kettle—and either may likely happen—I shall have had the satisfaction of feeling what it would be like if you were really my own girl, who would welcome me back if I should be so lucky as to escape tomahawk and bullet, and who would mourn for me should I fall." The light of a strong love illumined his brave, honest face as he spoke.

There was still silence. It was hard that at such a moment she should remain obdurate. His heart swelled to bursting ; she must be altogether heartless. Bras de Fer at last found courage to steal an anxious, imploring glance in the direction of his sweet tormentor. Nanon stood still as a statue ; the warm tears were streaming down her cheeks, but a strangely happy smile lingered about her lips.

" If you please, Master Baptiste Bras de Fer, but it is an innocent one may eat with salt, your Canadian." The color had returned to the girl's cheek, the sparkle to her eye. " Your wits have long been wool gathering ; say, then, is it possible that you have found them at last ? Did you expect the women to make love to you, my fine big fellow ? "

Du Chesne had drawn Lydia apart from the crowd. The girl made no effort to control herself ; sobbing convulsively, she clung to him as, taking her hands in his, his eyes went slowly over her from head to foot. He was silent, as one who, looking for the last time on a face he loves, would carry the memory of it with him to the wide world's end.

"Stay! Give the expedition up; let the others go. What does it matter? Even if the English come here, I may find friends among them. Do not leave me; the parting will kill me," she entreated.

The young Canadian shook his head. He scarcely understood her thought, or grasped the idea that she should dream of placing herself between him and his duty. A low, pitiful wail, like that of some helpless creature in distress, stole unawares from her quivering lips. Du Chesne shivered, and looked around fearfully. In all his life he had never endured torture like this; great drops of moisture gathered on his brow. Could courage desert him now? It was Diane who, rousing her dauntless spirit with courage that affection alone could give, came to his aid. She had reached the highest manifestation of human passion—self-sacrifice—and was learning that the soul can be taught to bear pain as the saints taught their bodies to bear the rigors of hardship and self-mortification. She was like a soldier who must fight till the last gasp, who must bear every blow like a stoic, so long as there was any excuse for the conflict.

"They call you, du Chesne; leave Lydia to my care. The Blessed Virgin protect you."

An expression of sharp anguish for a moment marred the composure of his countenance. A quick breath escaped him, half groan, half sob; one long, lingering look, and he was gone.

CHAPTER XXII.

THE DEPARTURE.

PIERRE LE BER and de Crisasi were standing side by side; the Chevalier was also to form one of the expedition. As Diane looked at the two men she was conscious of a pang of keen self-reproach. Had her girlish levity and thoughtlessness indeed made havoc of their lives? Her imagination endowed them with the pathos of her own suffering. Pierre was thin and haggard. He had drifted far from that state of acquiescent contemplation, passionless and impersonal, destitute of either desire or movement, which in the estimation of the mystic constitutes the highest conception of enduring bliss. A dreadful tension of resistance, a dim anguish of fear and impotence, had him in possession. His passion blinded him, but it could not stifle the abhorrence of the chains which bound him, nor could it restore his self-esteem. He seemed to have fallen to the lowest depths, yet this despairing dream was more exquisite than any of his mystical visions.

De Crisasi, on the contrary, in the perfection of his high breeding, was even blander and more courtly than ever. He was a strong man, who could calmly

set self aside and rise above the sensations of the
hour. The Indian witch's prediction, in his opinion,
had settled the whole affair. He had received his
death-warrant, and since all was so soon to be over, it
was really not worth while to trouble about mundane
matters. Life had been hard of late years, and this
very conflict would likely end all. He had always
desired a soldier's death ; he had a soldier's simple
faith, too, in the duty of obedience, courage and discipline, and made no question that fate had dealt hardly
with him. As Diane's glance met his, over her whole
frame there came a tremulous fluttering of apprehension, as though beneath the warmth of true affection
her self-control were breaking ; something inexpress-
ibly touching came into her eyes. That look over-
came the man who loved her. De Crisasi removed
his hat, and bowed profoundly.

" M. de Chevalier," the girl exclaimed impulsively,
" let me wish you God-speed. My prayers shall
follow you."

His heart leaped into his throat. Could it be
possible that his devotion had won its reward, that
the twilight of life should be gilded by a ray of vivid
sunshine? Then he smiled at the absurdity of his
own fancy. Two great hot tears, that scorched like
fire, gathered in Mademoiselle de Monesthrol's eyes,
and fell upon her cheeks unheeded.

" M. Le Chevalier, my cousin du Chesne carries
with him all our hopes, especially those of my uncle
and my poor Lydia. If it should happen to be in

your power to shield him from danger, I know we can rely upon you, our friend."

The Sicilian had given this girl the best love of his heart, yet their acquaintance had been at best but a formal one. His fancy had endowed her with many high qualities, but never before had he realized her tenderness and simple womanliness. He spoke in a low, moved tone.

" The confidence with which you have honored me, Mademoiselle, shall not be in vain. It is a soldier's fate to die with fortitude and resignation, professing the fate of a Christian. Du Chesne is my valued friend and comrade ; if any act of mine can avail to help him, to bring him back to those who love him, you can trust to me. The prayers of such as you, Mademoiselle, must ever be heard in heaven."

" Diane, hold up the little one, high, there, that his father's last look may rest upon his face. I can no longer see," pleaded Madame de St. Rochs, "and Armand must not see me weep."

" Diane, I can't bear it, I am fainting ; take me home." Sobbing and quivering, Lydia clung to her friend. " I am afraid of the Indians and the noise. Oh ! let us go away."

" For our Blessed Lady's sake try to comfort her," were du Chesne's parting words. " She is only a child, sensitive and tender-hearted, and it is I who have brought this sorrow upon her. For my sake be good to her, Diane."

"My daughter!"

As he looked upon his youngest son, Jacques Le Ber grasped his ward's arm. He spoke almost sternly. The strong muscles about his mouth quivered, though the facial lines did not lose their firm expression.

A soft golden haze, obscuring the view of the opposite shore, lay upon the river, sweeping on in subdued silvery tints. The Indians manned the large elm-bark canoes, their paddles cleaving the sunshine and dimpling the waters of the river. The savage voices arose in a wild tumult of resounding yells ; the soldiers cheered lustily; a sharp wailing cry resounded from the shore.

The agony of parting, the strain and stress of the hour at last over, du Chesne stood erect in the bow of his canoe. His handsome young face, eager and animated with the excitement of adventure, bore no trace of grief or care or doubt ; in the relief afforded by action all dark forebodings had sunk into the background. As the boats vanished from the tear-dimmed eyes that watched the last gleam of the receding oars, the strains of a stirring chorus resounded across the wave—

> "*Grand Dieu! sauvez le Roi.*
> *Grand Dieu! sauvez le Roi,*
> *Sauvez le Roi.*
> *Que toujours glorieux,*
> *Louis victorieux,*
> *Voit ses enemies,*
> *Toujours soumis.*"

CHAPTER XXIII.

SUSPENSE.

LE BER stood alone in the world, though surrounded by family ties and dependents. His individuality was so marked and striking that he had few close friends, though his commercial interests bound him to many associates. During this period of anxiety old griefs, seared over by time and distance, acquired fresh vitality to sting. Pierre, in his feverish unrest, had betaken himself to the hospital to pray; but it was not so much the fate of the colony, or anxiety for his brother's welfare, that troubled Le Ber's eldest son, as consternation concerning his own individual shortcomings. His sister was as remote from her father as though she had already attained that heaven which was the object of her thoughts and prayers. The merchant's spirit fainted for sore need of human help, human nearness. In this emergency it was the stranger that he had sheltered who clasped his hand, whispering bright words of cheer and encouragement, ever ready to offer sweet and gracious sympathy.

"You must learn to be brave, as becomes a soldier's bride, my sweet one," du Chesne had exhorted Lydia.

But the girl had no qualifications for ripening and mellowing under the influence of any searching mental experience. The atmosphere was antagonistic; she hated pain, longed for brightness, pined for sunshine. She was peevish and nervous, and had no idea of self-command; nor could she understand how it was that all the world was not absorbed in her affliction. That soft, flattering aspect of life in which she had delighted seemed to be receding from her. Diane's patience with her moods was unfailing, yet there was something about the French girl that awed Lydia and held her at a distance. Le Ber, who had conceived some suspicion that his long-dreamed-of plans for an alliance with the de Monesthrols might be frustrated by the presence of the English captive, looked upon her with cold disapproval. Whenever she dared, Nanon, whose sense of exasperation had reached fever point, jeered and flouted at the blonde beauty. Madame la Marquise, who had had excellent occasion for weeping bitterly many times in her life, declared that these ceaseless tears gave her the *migraine*.

"You will retire to your chamber, my daughter," the Marquise commanded, with a disdainful condescension which was not unkindly, looking down at the swollen, tear-stained face with a serene surprise, too elevated to partake of the nature of disgust. "You will have *tisane* for the sick—I have already commanded Nanon to prepare it—you will say your prayers and remain in seclusion. Where there are many anxious hearts we need cheer. There will be time for tears and lamentation when hope no longer exists, although even then I cannot see that lamentation is of use to ourselves or others. When the men are ready to give their lives for their faith and their country, it is the women's part to nerve and encourage them; what are our pitiful weaknesses that they should stand in the way of our duty? It is the right of the nobles to submit to the decrees of Providence, to subdue the body, to show ourselves models of cheerfulness and resignation, that the more ignorant may learn to follow our example. But why talk or reason with those who have no ears to hear and no spirit to learn the lesson? Therefore, my kitten, retire to your own apartment, where, at least, you will have no chance of afflicting others."

It must be admitted that the Marquise de Monesthrol was given to contemplating calamities with a courage which appeared overwhelming to less undaunted spirits.

Madame de St. Rochs, unable to endure the loneliness of her own home, determined to take up her abode at Le Ber's. She came rushing in impetuously, white, cold, and shivering, in the midst of the August heat, clasping the baby and a bundle, which seemed all one, so closely were they held. The childish creature threw herself at Diane's feet, clutching her friend's knees, still grasping the bundle and the little waxen baby, who never seemed alarmed, in the other arm.

"I cannot keep up alone any longer, and I am ashamed to let the others see me grieve. Let me be quiet—hide me, and don't let anybody look at me. Diane, tell me how I can live till news comes. I have fearful dreams; I cannot be strong like you."

"At the first touch of sorrow these children think they will die," mused the Marquise. "Ah! life were very simple could it end when it becomes unendurable. No; poor little Cecile, who is not without courage in her childish way, will live through it all, and will learn to suffer like a woman in the passion and patience of silence. But it is harder for those older, who, while feeling the wound, know that time will heal, and yet know that a look, a touch, a tone, will have power at any moment to revive the old agony till life ends. The happy delusions of youth find no resurrection."

Under the soothing influence of Diane's consoling presence, the baby wife succeeded in recovering her courage. As her spirits rose in transient reaction against the despondency which had crushed her, the absurd, hapless child committed a hundred extravagances. She chattered and laughed, played wild games with the baby and Nanon—pastimes which were at any moment in danger of being interrupted by vehement thunderstorms of despair.

"Our good friend Le Ber has afforded us protection; it is but right that we should share his anxiety," decided the Marquise.

Madame de Monesthrol's reception-room was continually thronged by women whose gaiety was almost reckless in its exuberance; but there remained an intent, listening look upon the vivacious French faces and sobs often struggled up surreptitiously amidst the laughter. While awaiting the decision of all those tremulous doubts and fears, they bravely endured the dreadful anxiety with which those shiver and burn whose strongest hopes hang in the balance. After all, most of these sorely tried people experienced a sort of desperate trust in circumstances; and the fact that duty was the thing to be considered, and not anybody's feelings, was cheerfully recognized.

For the demoiselle de Monesthrol, the old order of things had been completely overthrown. Deprived of affection and close sympathy, she was still looking out upon a world not realized, a bewildered spectator of something like the throes of creation, seeing the new landscape tumble and roll into place, the heights and hollows changing. Those about her had their own engrossing anxieties; no one thought of her save as a friendly and disinterested sympathizer. Whatever she endured she endured alone. Yet between every pang of heart sickness there intervened bright glimpses of wayward sunshine, stirrings of fresh, uncontrollable hope. Reserve forces of strength, hitherto unsuspected, developed under the strain of silent endurance. Only a supreme resolve could have steadied her nerves, calmed the fluttering pulses, and preserved self-command. An expression of collected strength that was becoming habitual, and that during life was never again to leave it, settled upon Diane's face. These few days had made the change of years. Her brow was contracted with lines hitherto unknown to its broad serenity, her eyes looked out eagerly from lids that had grown curved with anxiety, her mouth was drawn and colorless. Through all she tried to remind herself that God was still in heaven, faith and mercy on earth ; the joy of her youth had withered, but duty must teach her to be wise and strong and courageous.

"Blessed Mother of Sorrow, help me to bear through this hour—help me to endure the burden for half a day—let my strength hold out till night," prayed Diane de Monesthrol.

CHAPTER XXIV.

A PILGRIMAGE TO MOUNT ROYAL.

THE long anxious days that followed the departure of the troops, with little occupation save that of watching and waiting, with endless dreadful suggestions of what might be happening, were a severe ordeal to the whole settlement. It seemed as though a trifle might turn the balance—might mean ruin, total destruction of all hopes and plans, or, on the other hand, afford the blessed sweetness of relief.

With Diane the flame of suffering burned so fiercely that it permitted no rest. She could allow herself to look neither backward nor forward. Suddenly swept out of the joy of her youth into circumstances so desperate—waiting, dumb and steadfast, before the necessity which could not be resisted—there were moments of wild rebellion of spirit, paroxysms of impatience with life and its complications, a longing to escape this restless wretchedness, which was almost unbearable, alternating with brief, ecstatic moments of complete self-renunciation. What was the strength of her womanhood good for, the French girl asked herself, if not to teach her to tread with calm fortitude those dark paths which seem to be the

only way to heaven ; if not to afford solace to those
dependent upon her ministries, to lead her to endure,
with high heart and constancy, the buffets of fortune.

Three days had passed, and yet to Ville Marie, waiting in anxiety, no news had come.   M. de Valrenne
had promised to send a messenger directly he could
secure any tidings of the enemy's movements, and
many regarded this prolonged silence as ominous
of disaster.

The night of the third day was oppressively warm ;
the landscape lay wrapped in a soft incense-breathing
obscurity.   The feverish excitement tingling in Diane
de Monesthrol's veins drove away all thought of sleep.
Suspense imparted an unnatural keenness to all her
faculties, imagination was stimulated to the highest
point, fears and fancies thronged her excited brain.
Her pulses leapt with a prescient thrill of some blow
about to fall.   She was convinced that a supreme
crisis had arrived, the endurance of which would tax
her strength to the utmost.   It seemed as though, in
the midst of her gay and fearless career, she had been
caught in the gigantic iron hand of a ruthless Fate
that could not fail to crush her.

Suddenly her whole being seemed to contract and
shiver, with a nameless agony of apprehension.   She
could no longer endure the house, which seemed to
stifle her ; perhaps the cool night air might relieve this
overpowering horror.   Breathless, trembling, she
rushed out into the garden.   Over Mount Royal
the moon was shining in a cloudless sky, its sheen

lighting up the tin roof of Notre Dame until it shone like silver, illuminating the dark foliage of the quaint garden, and driving its lances of pearly light through the close-woven branches. Beneath the shade a sort of mystic twilight prevailed ; the dim trees rose in soft undulations half veiled in the faint and dreamy light. In the silent hush of nature the dew fell like a benediction ; all the breathings of night were suggestive of peace and balm.

Diane moved amidst the familiar scene with a dazed and bewildered consciousness that made all her surroundings appear like the dim reality of a dream. This ethereal twilight, with its pale, ineffable clearness, seemed to be the hour of tender reveries, of delicate visions. She heard, without heeding, a hundred crackling sounds—echoes, movements, the rustling of leaves, the occasional twittering of some bird disturbed in its nest. A depression deep and dark, the inevitable reaction succeeding a long strain of agitation, took possession of her. The feverish energy which had until now sustained her gave out, and with the physical exhaustion came the mental. All the pain and trouble of the last few days became focused into a haunting fear. It was one of those times when it seems possible for a human being to stand outside of material things ; when the veil which hides the everlasting verities is raised before eyes all pained and strained with gazing. The windows of Jeanne Le Ber's room, overlooking the garden, stood wide open to the summer breeze. An overwhelming impulse moved Diane. No longer able to stifle the cry of her anguish, she sank on her knees, stretching out imploring, passionate hands. Was it the moonlight, or the play of her own fancy, or did a slight, wasted form appear at the window, dreamily indistinct in the prevailing obscurity? Had the urgency of human need torn the saint from her prayers and her vigils? The girl's voice, clear and penetrating, echoed through the stillness.

"Have you, far away there, no feeling for our trouble? Even in the bliss of heaven itself it seems as though one's heart must be touched by love and grief and pain. You have sacrificed yourself for the country—cannot you help your own in their extremity? Du Chesne—he is your brother, if you can recall the ties of kindred where you are—du Chesne may be grievously wounded; he may even now be lying still in death. Have you ceased to hear, to feel? Does no woman's heart beat in your breast?"

Did a white face, with deep-sunken, haggard eyes look down upon her from the window—a face more like that of a dead woman than a living one? It seemed to the excited girl, driven to extremities by her own fancy as much as by stress of circumstances, that her cry fell upon a passionless, unseen world which returned no answer. There was a blighting silence, like a conscious death. A heavy, dull despair settled upon her.

"You are all alike, St. Joseph and the saints; you are content with your own goodness, and are dead

and deaf and dumb concerning the claims of earth;
but we others are only flesh, our hearts throb and
bleed and burn; we cannot keep silent. Du Chesne
is nothing to me but my old playmate, the companion
of my childhood; I have no claim upon him, he owes
me no duty—he never even guessed that I cared for
him. I merit suffering, I who dealt it out to others,
but why should he pay the penalty for my fault? I
have been pitiless, though I never meant it; the good
God may well be pitiless to me, but not to him, not
to him. If I could only tell the Chevalier that I
repent; I never thought my coquetry meant suffering, I regarded playing at love as a light jest." Diane
detailed her misdeeds in a voice of anguish. "And
Pierre, too, he might have been happy enough with
his prayers and his painting had I but let him alone;
but it amused me to try my power—the Holy Virgin
forgive me!—and this is the end. Du Chesne told
me that I did not know the meaning of true love. I
have learned too late. Of what use is your perfection, your credit at the court of heaven, your prayers
and virtues and mortifications, if you will not help
us? And I—I would rather be wicked and be able
to aid those I love, or at least to suffer with them."

For a time after this impassioned outburst she lay
hushed in exhaustion, then a new thought aroused
her to action.

'There is the mountain cross of M. de Maisonneuve; it is said that great graces have been obtained
there. We must lose no time. They might be fight-

ing even now, and this may be the moment of greatest danger."

"Lydia, Lydia, awaken! We will go to pray at the cross of M. de Maisonneuve."

The English girl lay sleeping with cheek upon her hand, like an innocent babe. The perfect repose of her position was so strangely childish and trustful that it was hard to realize she was slumbering on the brink of terror and desolation. The incongruity impressed Diane forcibly, but as she knelt beside the couch her face grew soft and womanly. When she felt her friend's hand laid gently on her shoulder, Lydia started up with a faint cry, rubbing her eyes and her soft flushed cheeks.

"Diane, why have you awakened me? When I am asleep I can at least forget," she protested, sitting up in bed, and staring at the demoiselle de Monesthrol as if she were not sufficiently awake to realize exactly what the scene meant. Diane's expression of restrained excitement recalled all; she flung herself down on the pillows, and broke into violent sobbing.

"Something has happened, news has come; I see by your face that it is evil tidings. The savages are upon us, and even if they come here to scalp me, I am too weak to move."

"No, no news has come, Lydia, but rise and dress," was the crisp, laconic reply. "We will go to the mountain cross to pray for du Chesne's safety. I have a conviction that at this moment he needs our prayers."

Lydia's blue eyes opened, wide and startled; in her consternation she forgot to sob.

"But it is dark night, still and lonely. The savages may line every foot of the way; we may be killed or taken prisoners. Oh! I dare not face the dangers," she cried, shuddering.

"The greater the merit of the pilgrimage. Our sufferings may enable us to obtain grace; for danger, I think nothing of it. Dress quickly and quietly; if we are observed, we shall not be allowed to start."

Action was a relief from pain, and Diane was bestirring herself vigorously. Finding herself being hastily dressed, against her will, and perceiving that her peevish importunities produced absolutely no effect, Lydia ceased to resist. Indeed, this pale girl with a troubled restlessness in her anxious eyes, a pathetic droop of the red lips, moving with a steady purpose, bore so little resemblance to vivid, brilliant Diane, that the English girl was thoroughly frightened, and became passive in the hands of the stronger spirit.

A pilgrimage to the mountain cross was considered at Ville Marie a fashionable act of devotion. As the way to the mountain teemed with real and tangible dangers, ladies generally undertook it in parties, protected by armed escorts. Every tree or stone might be expected to offer shelter to feathered and painted enemies; there were also wild beasts to be dreaded; so that in starting there was always the possibility of not being able to return.

Soon the two girls—Diane erect and stately, never for an instant pausing or faltering ; Lydia clinging feebly to her arm—like shadows moving amidst shadows, were traversing the deserted streets. The desolate, dark night was full of visionary terrors and real dangers. The chant of the St. Lawrence filled the air, the river trembling with violet tints and glancing pearly shafts. Presently they crossed a swiftly flowing stream, and emerged upon the open country. Here no vagrant echo, not even the stir of a leaf, disturbed the stillness. The dew was rich with cool fragrance. Now dark trees would close up the path, then it would widen into a world of space as it passed into the odorous moorland or crossed little rivulets tinkling on their way to the river. The moonbeams, piercing through the interlacing branches, threw chequered shadows on the path. Anon, amidst vistas of leafy shade, they caught fleeting glimpses of the illuminated world beyond.

As the two girls crept up the slope, under the flickering shadows of the trees, the scene was incredibly solitary and mournful. The path, simply an Indian trail, was long and toilsome. Vegetation was dense, tangled with vines, sombre with gloomy foliage, through which the white light strove to penetrate. Lydia, whose feelings were impressions which rarely deepened into emotion, was rendered helplessly hysterical by terror. All Diane's faculties were absorbed in a sombre, bewildering excitement, as with the English captive sobbing, panting, clinging to her arm, she made her way through the thicket. Before long she was obliged to support the almost fainting girl. Little did it matter what they endured, if their sufferings might perchance gain the grace to save the young Canadian from a cruel fate. Once the long dewy trail of a creeper caught Diane lightly like the grasp of a restraining hand ; a soft rustle among the leaves caused the heart to leap in her breast ; that long-drawn cry of a bird which broke the stillness in melancholy cadences might be the signal of danger.

At last, gleaming white amidst dark, glossy foliage, arose the cross erected on Mount Royal in a vow to God for the conversion of the savages. Lydia, over-come by fatigue, fear, the night air, the strain and agitation of the expedition, now sank down against a boulder. She had ceased to reason, and only desired rest. The wooded gray slope towered immu-tably above them, the wind harping in the pines. The moon had dropped below the horizon, familiar objects acquired strangely grotesque forms in the uncertain light, while in the blue sky above trembled a single luminous star. Pressing on, Diane knelt at the foot of the cross. It seemed as though she had at length reached a sure refuge, a power to whose strength and goodness she could confidently appeal. Then her hands clenched and her whole frame began to shake.

"It is for du Chesne, for his life, that we have come so far to pray. He is so young and strong ; he might be so happy. Holy Virgin Mother, who knowest the secret of all love and suffering, I ask nothing for myself; let me suffer, but spare him." The sound of her voice seemed to profane the hush of nature. Its tones had acquired a husky shrillness in which there was a note of presaging horror.

"They are too holy, the saints—they despise earthly pains and losses—they think only of their own heavenly bliss—they set themselves against us. Oh! how can they look calmly on our suffering? God in heaven, have mercy! or is He also too high and great to care for our poor, miserable concerns? I will sacrifice myself—my life—what does anything matter? If he returns in safety I make a vow to enter the Congregation as a novice, to devote myself to the expiation of my sins; only spare him, oh, God!" Diane writhed and battled for air as a paroxysm of suffocating sobs came upon her; then, worn out with wild heart-broken weeping, she lay at the foot of the cross, motionless and exhausted.

CHAPTER XXV.

TIDINGS AT LAST.

AS the girls crept wearily homeward, the first rays of the summer dawn were breaking in the east in flushes of saffron and pink ; overhead the sky held quivering lights, ready to flash into a blaze. A refreshing sense of physical renewal was in the cool blueness of the morning ; there was dewy fragrance in the atmosphere ; the trees gave out a breath of strength, the golden-rod gleamed in the hollows, the heights were purple bronze. Lydia moved in a state of passive exhaustion, half stupefied. As they reached home Diane turned to her companion a face which glowed with some subtle inspiration.

"Be assured that du Chesne is safe. God is good. Oh, behold! that must be a messenger from M. du Plessis, sent by M. de Callière. See how all the people are gathering to hear what the tidings may be. You are so exhausted, Lydia, it were perhaps better to retire to your room. I see my uncle. I will go to him ; he will certainly know what has occurred. If there is news I will return to you." An instant later she had joined Le Ber on the shore.

"Is there news of M. de Valrenne's command ?"

"Yes, news has come at last. Oshawa has been sent to say that they have caught sight of the enemy. M. de Callière lies ill at La Prairie. M. de Valrenne is stationed between there and Chambly." Jacques Le Ber showed no sign of weakness save a momentary trembling of the lines about the mouth.

"Oh! my uncle, even to-night they may be with us victorious."

The trader smiled. It would never do to admit the possibility of disaster.

"The sky may brighten for New France, my daughter. I have ever remarked that good as well as ill-luck runs in courses. Our good fortune may now commence."

A number of women, who had been attending the early mass, were emerging from the church of Notre Dame. Among them, erect and stately, walked Madame de Monesthrol, attended by Nanon and followed by Madame de St. Rochs with her baby in her arms. Pierre, thin and dark and sallow, pushed his way through the crowd to where the demoiselle de Monesthrol stood a little apart.

"Diane, I have here for you a picture of Our Lady of Pity surrounded by the five wounds of her Son." He tried to fortify himself by recalling the excellence of his intention, but that only increased his nervous agitation. "I have been holding a neuvena in honor of St. Joseph and all the holy saints. For nine days, a number especially dedicated to the holy angels, have I prayed, and no light has dispersed the dark-

ness of my soul. Dazzling visions, the creation of
the Father of Evil, ever appear before my eyes.
Instead of the angelic faces which once beamed upon
me, it is thine I see, glorified by the crown of
martyrdom."

Until now Diane had had slight patience with
Pierre's freaks and fancies, considering them effemi-
nate and unreasonable. Now, looking at him with
wistful eyes, she said quietly :

" Dear Pierre, we are all sorely tried by anxiety and
suspense. Try to forget your own temptations, my
cousin, in thought for others. Could you not support my uncle, who is alone in this time of trouble ?
On every hand you will find those who have need of
your kindly ministrations."

In the young man's impatient gesture there appeared all the petulance of misery. He felt it unreasonable and monstrous that anything save the
painful state of his own concerns should occupy
Diane's mind.

" I stand alone," he complained. " My father is
absorbed in worldly interests ; your heart is engrossed
by vanity. What are the trivial affairs of this life—
privation, danger, and even death—in comparison
with the perils that menace the soul ? "

The next day a terrible storm broke over Ville
Marie. Great trees groaned and snapped like
saplings in the blast, the wind raved, the whole
heavens were illumined by the swift electric flashes.

Such a storm had never been known in the colony.
Nature, in her convulsive throes smote the stoutest
heart with terror. Late in the afternoon the tempest
ceased. The sun set fair and beautiful, with rays of
purple and gold smiling on the waters of the river;
the clouds, black with the recoil of tempest, gradually
broke into rifts, trailing silvery tints of celestial hue,
sublime marvels of color.

Diane joined Le Ber as he walked down to the shore.
That day no news had been received, yet it was almost certain that an engagement had taken place.
His face was grey with consuming care; his eyes had
a famished expression. The demoiselle de Monesthrol slipped her hand within the arm of her guardian
and walked quietly by his side, offering a mute responsive sympathy which was grateful to his soul.

"We shall surely have news before night, my
daughter. Behold M. du Plessis on the shore; like
ourselves, he looks for tidings from our men."

Restless expectation tinged everybody's thoughts.
These were anxious moments to the French commander. No one understood better than he the
reality of the danger that threatened the settlement.
His brow was heavy with care, though he endeavored
to seem at ease.

As she looked out upon the shining waters of the
river, a strange perception came to Diane de Monesthrol. It seemed as though the world had broken
into fragments and lay crumbling at her feet, while
her spirit soared free above the ruins. She already

understood the tragic possibilities of fear and loss
and pain; she had acknowledged the necessity of
devotion, self-abnegation, heroism; now a lightning
flash of intuition revealed to her the terrible beauty of
self-sacrifice, giving her to realize, though faintly and
indistinctly, some conception of a divine help, offered
with a human eagerness of sympathy, patient until
the feeble mortal hands could reach up and lay hold
of it. With this conviction a wonderful peace came
to succeed the burning wretchedness. Just then the
peals of the Angelus rang out, echoing through the
mountain slopes and over the waters. It was the
voice of prayer and praise, rising in triumph above all
earthly passions of grief and pain.

Groups of women, with heavy eyes and care-worn
faces, holding their rosaries with fingers which still
mechanically pressed the beads as they walked, while
their lips moved in silent prayer, came out from the
dusky seclusion of the church, where day and night
lights burned and prayers were offered. The beadle of
the Parish Church, in full uniform, mace in hand, was
narrating with much dramatic emphasis all the particulars of a supposed engagement, to a keenly
interested group of listeners, when the tide of his
eloquence was abruptly checked by a sharp poke in
the ribs that deprived him of breath. Nanon, her
face flushed like a peony, the lappets of her cap
flying, swept past like a whirlwind.

" *Seigneur dieu!* I would know the truth, me, after
waiting so long—a canoe!"

"A boat arriving!—tidings!—tidings!" The words passed from one to another, and were repeated in a variety of keys, as, moved by a common impulse, the group rapidly dispersed, flying down to the shore, where the whole population of the town seemed to have gathered.

Propelled by four strong arms, skimming lightly as foam over the surface of the water, leaving a faint track behind it as it moved, the frail craft advanced. As it came between the eager spectators and the sun, the forms of those it contained stood out like silhouettes against the light. The citizens of Ville Marie waited with quickened breath and beating hearts, hoping, fearing, expecting—they dared not think what. Le Ber gazed with the wrinkles deepening on his brow. The setting sun shone so brilliantly in his eyes that he raised his hand to shade them, and for the moment could see nothing.

"Le Canotier and Madouaska—the Blessed Virgin send us good news," du Plessis announced hurriedly, speaking with a catch in his breath.

Then again a breathless silence settled on the crowd ; not a sound was heard but the dipping of the paddles and the soft murmur of the waves as they caressed the shore. Silently, swiftly the canoe advanced. Beside the Canotier was an Indian, a tall, superbly built man, whose remarkably regular features might have been sculptured out of Florentine bronze. Over his shoulders was thrown a mantle of caribou skin with pink and lilac border. His head was shaved, with the exception of a tuft on the crown, which was ornamented with hawk feathers, resembling the crest of an antique helmet. His face was absolutely impassive in its immobility. As the canoe grated on the shore, a dozen willing hands offered aid in landing her.

"All is well?" cried du Plessis, unable longer to restrain his anxiety. Then a shuddering, convulsive sob ran through the ranks of the women as a French officer appeared, bearing, in haggard eye and ghastly pallor, traces of the fatal wound which was rapidly draining his life-blood. Tender hands lifted him from the boat.

"It is M. le Capitaine de Breteuil. He is dying!"

The women separated to allow a lady, with three little children clinging to her gown, to push her way to the front.

"Carry him home," she said quietly. "At least the good Lord has granted the favor of permitting him to die with me. I must have courage; he will need me beside him. Let us be together while we may."

For an instant she had seemed on the point of breaking into a wild outcry, but quickly checking the impulse, had braced herself for the duty waiting her. Now, as she spoke, the icy composure of voice and manner seemed almost like indifference. A black-robed nun silently detached herself from the crowd, and placed herself at the side of the stricken wife. Dollier de Casson, his brown earnest face all quivering with emotion, solemnly raised his hands in benediction over the living and the dying.

"You will not grudge the sacrifice, my daughter? It is a hero willingly and gallantly laying down his life for his faith and his King."

"There will be plenty of time to consider that later," she answered, very quietly. "Now he needs me. I have no thought to spare for aught else."

The whole assembly were hanging eagerly upon the accents of le Canotier, who had already delivered the despatches he had brought to M. du Plessis.

"We marched straight to Chambly—such were our orders. The object of M. de Valrenne was to permit those devils of English to pass, and then, by placing himself in their rear, to cut them off from their canoes. Our scouts—and there are none better than Misti, Tshinespek and Mushawana,—soon discovered the advance of the enemy, and then we marched six or seven miles towards La Prairie, on the path by which Schuyler was retreating. The sun stood high; it was nine o'clock when our scouts met those of the foe, and then—*Dianthe!*—the woods resounded with the shrill yells of the Indians as their war-whoops gave the alarm. You all know how that part of the country is buried in forests. We take possession of a ridge of ground that crosses the way of those English wolves. Two enormous trees thrown down by the storm have fallen along the crest of this rising ground, and behind these we crouch in a triple row, well hidden by bushes and thick standing stumps, like wolves ready to spring upon their prey. Believe me, Mesdames and Messieurs, I have witnessed much of forest warfare, yet never before have I seen so hot a conflict. The English charged like devils—(to give them their due they do not lack courage)—and were sent reeling back by a close and deadly volley. Like hail the balls flew—three times were we mingled together, scorching each other's shirts by the flash of our guns. With still greater fury our enemies repeated the attack, and dislodged us from our place of ambush. It was then the veritable struggle commenced. Figure to yourself that they determined to break through our lines, and our commandant desired, above all else, to drive them back within the reach of our people at La Prairie. Our muskets thirsted to kill. There, amidst that storm of hell-fire, stood M. de Valrenne, giving his orders, calm and smiling as at a ball. Forty dead they left behind them, those English, yet they managed to cut their way through and drive us from the path."

To the anxious listeners the prospect appeared to grow darker and more appalling. There had been a sharp engagement, many lives apparently had been lost, and who could divine whose heart had been smitten, whose home rendered desolate?

"M. le Lieutenant Dumerque?" asked a timorous voice.

"Dead; shot at my side," responded le Canotier, with the sharp brevity of excitement. "I see a little officer with hair as red as his coat, fighting like a Turk. I send him a sugar plum—*v'là!*—his legs in the air, but not before mon Lieutenant had fallen, pierced by a shot from his hand."

There was a faint stifled cry. A pale young girl, who had been listening eagerly, fell on the ground in a nerveless heap; an elderly woman, with face set in lines of stony composure, bent anxiously over her; then Dollier de Casson, raising the slight form in his strong arms, bore her away to her home.

"It is Mademoiselle Adèle de Montigny; they were to have been married in the early days of September. And his mother—it is the fourth son she has lost."

It seemed that those who listened to the vivid recital could see the dim forests and floating smoke-wreaths, with vague glimpses of the hidden foe. They could imagine the incessant rattle of musketry, could see terrible figures looming through the haze, and watch the gleaming of the war-axes as the weapons fell clattering from stricken hands.

CHAPTER XXVI.

DU CHESNE'S RETURN.

"AND M. de St. Rochs?"

Cecile was clinging to Diane's gown, trembling, shivering, half believing herself already a widow, the soft outlines and fresh bloom of youth contrasting oddly with the pathetic trouble of her eyes.

"M. de St. Rochs was safe, Madame, when I left. I was sent away in charge of mon Capitaine before the, fight was fairly over."

Like a little tempest, Madame de St. Rochs rushed into Diane's arms, sobbing, laughing, uttering inarticulate exclamations of joy.

Le Ber's grasp on his ward's arm tightened. She understood that he desired her to ask the question which his own lips could not frame. Twice Diane tried to speak, but her throat seemed to close each time; the words would not come. It was Cecile who, in a burst of joyful confidence, found voice for the consuming desire of the French girl's heart.

"And M. Le Ber du Chesne—he is safe, of course?"

"Ah! yes, Madame, our brave young commandant.

237

And is it any wonder that the bluecoats love their leader? He fought like all the king's troops in one, being of a valor truly marvellous."

The father caught his breath sharply and drew a hand across his eyes, as if to clear his mind from confused ideas. Diane had been watching the working of le Canotier's scarred and weather-beaten face with vigilant scrutiny. The reaction, the sweetness of relief, was almost as poignant a sensation as pain. For an instant she closed her eyes and clung to Le Ber's arm. With what trembling thanksgiving she welcomed this gleam of hope. The Blessed Virgin had granted her prayer; the Holy Mother had a woman's heart, and was touched by compassion. Though du Chesne would never be hers, yet he would live; his career, in the brilliancy of its promise, would not be cut short; he would continue to move in the light of God's earth; she would be spared the supreme anguish of yielding him up to death.

Absorbed in the interest of le Canotier's narrative, and in the incidents attending it, no one perceived the rapid advance of another canoe. The shrill voice of a child proclaimed the fact.

" *Voilà!* yet another canoe," exclaimed one of the group. "Truly, more news. It is M. le Chevalier and the Sieur d'Ordieux—yes, and Baptiste Bras de Fer."

Le Ber, turning abruptly, withdrew his support. Diane, gazing but not seeing, sickened with a sudden sense of dread. She made a hasty step forward, staggering like one blind, then, stretching her hands with a long, gasping cry, that seemed to carry with it the trouble of those last terrible days, recovered herself by a supreme effort.

"Mademoiselle, I have failed in my commission, believe me, through no negligence or fault of mine. I have brought back my brave and faithful comrade. Do me the justice to believe that I would willingly have given my own life in his stead." It was the Chevalier de Crisasi who spoke, the disorder of his dress showing plainly the desperateness of the conflict through which he had passed.

In the midst of this sudden panic, the downfall of all her hopes, Diane had pity to spare for him who felt so much. As he encountered her gaze he bowed his head reverently. At that moment the girl's secret was revealed to him, and the Sicilian gentleman stood awed and abashed before the revelation.

"It was but now they said he was safe; it cannot be du Chesne." Le Ber's shock was so great that he looked piteously into his ward's eyes as she stood with her white lips pressed together.

Diane's agitation affected her strangely. She was surprised at her own composure in this supreme crisis. Hastily forming a distinct plan of action, she coolly took command, directing everything. For the first terrible interval she could not even wonder, or doubt, or question. She seemed to have known it all long ago, to have felt the cold creeping to her heart to thrill her with a shiver as of ice, to have grown used and deadened to it. It was du Chesne who was being borne away helpless in Bras de Fer's strong arms, surrounded by anxious comrades and kindred—du Chesne, whose eyes were pathetic with the silent protest of life against death, whose bright, boyish face wore that mysterious expression, sweeter, calmer than a smile, that sometimes comes to those who look their last upon life. She saw Cecile drop down to the ground, heard Nanon's noisy grief, was conscious of the stricken look of Le Ber's face, yet she seemed to stand outside and beyond it all.

With the hush and awe of natural sympathy, friends and neighbors gathered around, looking with deep pity on the bereavement which might so easily have been their own. Ville Marie was overcast with mourning for the fate of the kindly, genial young fellow.

There was one whom the young Canadian sought —his wandering glances revealed the secret. All the force within Diane was torn two ways, so sorely rent as to scarcely leave her any strength for decisive action. Her own affection, jealous, restless, imperative, had claims which were irresistible. At such a moment who would remember the helpless stranger's rights ? Not Le Ber, who was absorbed in grief for the destruction of his hopes ; not Madame de Mones-throl, who despised the English captive's weakness ; nor Pierre, engrossed in his prayers and penances ; neither could it be Madame de St. Rochs, nor Nanon, both of whom had conceived violent prejudices against

the intruder. During all the years of her after life
Diane could never think of the strength of that
dreadful temptation without a convulsion of her
whole being. She had no choice ; the steadfast spirit,
holding brave sovereignty over the body and its
pangs, must triumph. Hearts, apparently, were made
to be crushed and broken. A little more or less,
what did it matter in the vast and silent anguish that
consumed her ? In the heat of conflict there came
a new tide in her veins, a novel force to all her
thought. It was she who must break the news of
this bereavement to her rival, and she would be
required to comfort and sustain. It must be her part
to see that du Chesne's desire was satisfied, that the
English girl should take her rightful place at her
lover's death-bed. Every trace of color died out of
Lydia's face as she listened ; she turned on Diane a
wild and appealing look.

"But it is not true ; it cannot be true. We were
to have been so happy together," she insisted desperately, sobbing out the words in her anguish and
terror.

In one of those brilliant impulses of generosity,
courage and self-sacrifice which bear a noble soul on,
heedless of the temptations of the body, to the performance of lofty deeds—acts of heroism in which life
goes for nothing—Diane supported the pretty, frightened creature who clung to her panting and sobbing.

"You will come to him. You will try to be calm
for his sake," the demoiselle de Monesthrol urged.

But Lydia was overwhelmed with fear. The shock rendered her helpless and hysterical; she wanted to force her own complaints and grievances upon the attention of others, rather than yield to the claims of the dying man. She was utterly unable to collect her scattered faculties. This frail sufferer, with spectral eyes and pain-distorted form, seemed to have no connection with her gay and gallant young lover. She loved strength, brightness, the joy of life, and hated anything that was maimed or gloomy. She shuddered involuntarily as a feeling of repulsion crept over her; she could not look at him without whitening and shivering. She was not touched by the spectacle of a valor so steadfast, a submission so sweet; her one thought was to escape the horror of it.

Du Chesne lay in a quiet room, while the moments which no human will could arrest swept on. He had accepted the verdict passed upon him as the most natural thing in the world—"quite simple," as he said.

He was still so young and ardent of temperament that even the dark passage to the grave abounded in hopeful portents. He would insist upon being propped up in bed, and being allowed to talk. Affection banished the solemn, wistful look from his face, and gleamed like faint flashes of sunshine from the edges of the dark shadow.

The young Canadian was tender and considerate, even on his death-bed. He was wondrously patient

in his pity for Lydia's simplicity and weakness; his
dying eyes followed her ceaselessly, with a faithful
love which had been born on earth, but which would
last forever.

Cecile, outside the door of the sick-room, cried out,
launching furious, vehement invectives against the
cruelty of Fate; and Nanon, all glowing red, her eyes
blazing with indignation, her lips quivering with genuine distress, stood by, with a gaze of wrath and
disgust fixed on the stranger's face.

But Lydia was too completely absorbed in her own
fright and misery to be sensible of criticism, ani-
mosity, or even the evidences of tenderest affection.
All her complacent little vanities had vanished as,
clinging to her friend with piteous, shaking hands,
she sought vainly to obtain some inspiration from the
desperate bravery of Diane's face.

"Diane, be good to her," pleaded the dying man.
"You are her only protector. You are strong and
tender and loyal. I can trust you, my brave and
faithful sister."

In the constancy of her courage Diane never either
faltered or failed. If she was crushed beneath the
cross which was laid upon her, she at least tasted the
supreme blessedness of sacrificing self. Tender affection gave sight to her eyes, and taught her how to
comfort and solace the sufferer, to beguile the pain
and tedium of a death-bed, to staunch those wounds
for which human art has no remedy.

A consciousness came over the household that sad

change and revolution hung over the family. Jean
Le Ber du Chesne was going away in the bloom of
his days to that unknown bourn of which God alone
knows the secret. It was very quiet in the death-
chamber, where the young hero lay looking at the
distant tapers, the one centre of light in the great
gloomy room, gazing with eyes from which all conflict had departed, abstracted in their wistfulness.
He had grown calm in absolute self-surrender, giving
a sigh occasionally to what might have been, and
feeling perhaps an awakening thrill of anticipation of
what was to come. The room was filled with dusky,
wavering shadows. On a *prie-dieu* close at hand
knelt Diane. The torture of one who had fought
a protracted battle was ended by the hard-won victory over self. In this solemn hour she felt the
stirring of some wider, grander life within, and the
human eyes gazed appealingly across the darkness
of present things, striving to see, no matter how indistinctly, the first faint glimmer of that light which
glows beyond the grave. Farther from the bed, two
nuns of the Congregation, Sister Marguerite Bourgeois, an aged woman whose serenity of countenance
was like a benediction, and sister Berbier, Superior
of the Convent of the Congregation, whispered together.

Something stirred softly. At the sound of the
measured, ill-assured movements, timid yet rushing,
with a definite pupose underlying the desperate haste,
even Diane raised her head, and the nuns, crossing

themselves, drew closer together. A wan, hollow-eyed form, gliding from among the shadows, advanced towards the bed, stood for a moment gazing down upon du Chesne's peaceful face, and then disappeared as noiselessly as it had entered. The strong and subtle tie of kindred had drawn Jeanne Le Ber from the seclusion of years. The spectators were awed by the sight of a mortal, divided from all human hopes and interests, yet still firmly bound to its inheritance of human woe.

Night had passed. The stars paled in the sky, lingering shadows dispersed, the dawn was breaking in the east. Sister Berbier rose, and crossing the room, threw open the heavy wooden shutters. The fresh, cool air, moist and odorous, rushed in ; and with it a searching ray of light, clear and terrible, fell upon the calm dead face on the pillow.

CHAPTER XXVII.

A COMPLETED SACRIFICE.

" MY daughter, when the earthly hope that lights existence has faded, and we find it impossible to lay down our lives to perish in the grave beside it—when we can neither endure our trouble nor be reconciled to it—we can only disengage ourselves and leave it behind us, dead and buried. The true and genuine portion of our sorrow lives ; the base regrets we must learn to cast from us ; there is no companionship between the living and the dead," Dollier de Casson assured Diane.

All had come to an abrupt and ruthless end ; the anxiety and suspense had terminated in dread certainty. Hope and fear had perished with du Chesne, yet the tense throb of anguish survived. The girl was crushed under the cross which had been laid upon her, and which she did not know how to bear. Pleasure and hope had broken off short ; existence was a solitude. Often it struck her as strange that no one had ever suspected that she, as well as the gallant young Canadian, had died.

Lydia's forlorn condition attracted much sympathy ; the sentimental appreciation of a dramatic situation, so dear to the French heart, operated in her favor. She enjoyed posing as a victim of affliction, and performed the role so modestly and gracefully that she won all hearts. Du Chesne to her would remain a tender, pensive memory, which throughout her life would be capable of affording occupation for an idle hour, comfort for a distressed one, and which would not forbid consolation.

Two years later, the Sieur d'Ordieux, by the death of his uncle, became Duke de Ronceval, and triumphed over his enemies. Though he had entered upon a great inheritance, and become a peer of France, the pompous little man was faithful in his attachments. He did not forget those who had befriended him in the day of adversity; his heart remained true to the woman whom he had loved with all the devotion of which he was capable.

The future of her niece had furnished the consuming anxiety of Madame de Monesthrol's existence. If her protector Le Ber should die, what would become of the beautiful portionless girl? If Diane only had a vocation, that would simplify matters; she might become a nun, and a safe retreat would be secured from the perils of the world. But Diane had no vocation, and the Duke de Ronceval's affection offered a solution of the difficulty.

When an advantageous settlement was in question, it was not the custom in those days to consult the bride's taste. The sacrifice of the individual for the good of the race was then—as it still to a large extent remains—a generally accepted principle among the French. A well-bred damsel, trained in the traditions of the ancient *régime*, would make it a point of honor to accept the fate which her family chose for her, just as a high-spirited girl of our generation would take a pride in rendering herself independent.

Youth and hope had perished, but the claims of duty remained imperative; so when Madame de Monesthrol urged, "By marrying the Duke you will not only secure a great establishment for yourself; you will also purchase peace for me. When I know that you are provided for, I can spend my last days in repose. I have suffered, my child, you will never know how much"—Diane could not turn a deaf ear to the prayer of the kinswoman who loved her well.

The annual ship was returning to France, an event always of the deepest importance to the whole colony. Every man, woman, and child who could manage to get to the water-side at Quebec, gathered to view the departure.

The most prominent passengers were the Duke and Duchess de Ronceval. Curled, powdered and decorated, the nobleman stormed at his obsequious lackeys, or gesticulated wildly as he jested with his friends. The pale, beautiful bride was composed and dignified. Madame de Monesthrol remarked with satisfaction that her niece bore herself with an air of the very highest distinction.

A little desolate group had gathered about Diane. This parting meant the sundering forever of ties which had been very close and dear. Jacques Le Ber was there. He had aged, and the stern lines of his face were visibly deepened. Madame de Monesthrol, older, frailer, always bearing her infirmities with suave dignity, leaned upon his arm. Nanon, her comely honest face disfigured by the tears which she made no effort to restrain, pressed close to her mistress.

"The sunshine of my life goes with thee." Le Ber spoke in a low, moved voice.

"It is your desire that I should serve your interests at the Court, my uncle."

"My little one, could I but accompany thee!" Then the Marquise added brightly, "Though the journey is beyond my strength, I can always pray for thy welfare. I can think of thee as occupying thy rightful place in the world, and I can praise the good God that the desire of my heart has been realized. Thy marriage has removed the last trace of anxiety from my mind; I can await my end in peace. Thy duty lies before thee, my daughter. Let no remembrance of a feeble old woman, whose stormy life is ending in a haven of rest, weaken thy peace. Think of me always as rejoicing in thy prosperity."

As the good ship *Renommée* disappeared below the horizon, Nanon lifted up her voice and wept with boisterous vehemence.

"When I looked my last look upon my demoiselle her face was like that of an angel. Never shall I see

the like again. My little one, that I cradled in my
arms, and who loved me with her whole heart. I am
but of the people—if my heart is broken I have no
need to look like a stone ; now that she has left me I
shall please myself by weeping like a waterspout.
She said to me, speaking, oh ! so gently, at the very
last, ' It is thy duty to stay with Madame, to comfort
and care for her, as it is mine to leave her. Neither
of us must forget her obligations, we will both strive
to fulfil them nobly and faithfully, good and loving
Nanon.' Oh ! my brave and beautiful demoiselle, I
coveted greatness for her, I wanted to see her set high
above all the world, and behold ! Her Grace Madame
la Duchess de Ronceval is taken away from my
sight. It sounds well, that title, even if my heart is
broken. How can I live without her? what can the
blessed saints be thinking of up in heaven there?
Behold that blonde English sheep, selfish and cold-
blooded as a snake, the happy wife of M. de Gallifet,
no less ! No one will ever cry her eyes out for her."

At the Court of Louis the Magnificent, Diane de
Ronceval lived out the years that remained to her.
The vivifying breath of an utterly unselfish affection
had touched her. All egotism had been annihilated
by the fierce sweep of a spiritual flame, before which
every unworthy desire and ambition had perished.
In the midst of a corrupt society, she preserved a
noble and lofty ideal. With an earnest and simple
contriving of gentle charities, she strove to make

some rough places smooth. Brave with the inspiration of faith and hope, she found happiness in identifying herself with the needs and claims of others.

If she were conscious of a wound which throbbed and bled, of unquenchable longings, of memories which never were to be forgotten, she contrived to carry her cross in such fashion that no other heart should be saddened, no other's joy shadowed. And the world was purer and brighter for one woman's faith and courage.

THE END.

www.ingramcontent.com/pod-product-compliance
Lightning Source LLC
Chambersburg PA
CBHW031428020726
47499CB00005B/1637